"I don't understand."
Frances was puzzled

"It's quite obvious you don't," Felix cut in. "Or else you wouldn't have let Mark Lucas come anywhere near you while I'm around."

"You know Mark?" she whispered incredulously.

"I should. He's married to my sister, Jessica!" Felix looked down at her stunned face. "Quite a coincidence, isn't it? And for God's sake stop playing the innocent. I know all about you and Mark at Chichester."

A wave of color swept over her face, and then went, leaving it ashen. "I...I can explain, Felix. Honestly, it's not what you think."

"No? Can you deny that Mark Lucas was willing to leave his wife because of you?"

She could not deny it, of course, and her face told him so.

Scorpio Summer

by

JACQUELINE GILBERT

Harlequin Books

TORONTO•LONDON•NEW YORK•AMSTERDAM
SYDNEY•HAMBURG•PARIS•STOCKHOLM

Original hardcover edition published in 1979
by Mills & Boon Limited
ISBN 0-373-02308-1
Harlequin edition published January 1980

For my sister Pamela Jean

Printed in U.S.A.

CHAPTER ONE

THERE was a sharp, biting wind blowing relentlessly down Regent Street, and the sun, appearing bravely for a few minutes, was very welcome, even though it was pale and weak. Snowdrops and crocuses were providing splashes of shy colour among the winter greenery, and daffodil yellow was promised in the bursting fat buds being buffeted to and fro in the public gardens.

Frances Heron lifted her face to the feeble sunshine, and quickening her step, thought with pleasure of spring. At this moment in time she felt an affinity for the coming season, for spring's message of new life and hope was also her motto for the day. The excitement bubbling away inside her was bursting to grow, rather like those daffodil buds, and this was evidenced by the way she walked, upright and confident, and by the eager set of her head.

The cause of this excitement was lying in her pocket now, a hastily written letter from her apartmentmate, Zoe Aleksander. Frances pushed her hand into her pocket and fingered the paper, which was fine-textured and expensive, the kind Zoe always used, and remembered the wording . . .

'Frankie—have heard from an influential source that London South are auditioning today, two-thirty, at their Edgware Road studios! Actress with Cornish accent required. Ask for a Tom Deverell. Best of luck! Zoe.'

Trust Zoe to have an influential source! thought Frances, with an inward grin, and as for luck—well, she was going to need it. Luck played an important role at auditions, she'd found that out very early on in her career. The thumbs down sign could be for any number of reasons, and none of them to do with ability. But she wouldn't think of failure ... somehow the day felt promising. Because of Zoe's influential source she wasn't now doing the dreary rounds of the agencies looking for work, but was going after something definite ... with a Cornish accent.

A smile played on her lips as she thought back longingly to all those early years spent in that part of England, the extreme south-west corner. Travelling with her doctor father on his daily rounds in the school holidays, exploring the cliffs between Sharpnose and Hartland Point with her friends, or tramping Bodmin Moor with her mother, picnicking by Trethevy Quoit or searching Brown Willie Tor for wild flowers and fossils for her mother's botany class. No ... a Cornish accent shouldn't give her much trouble!

For a moment, a wave of sadness swept over her as she remembered the closeness and the sense of belonging that came from being part of a family. An orphan for ten years, Zoe's parents were the nearest she had to family now, and made her very welcome with a warmth that their daughter had inherited, but it wasn't the same as having a family of your own.

Frances shrugged off these retrospective memories firmly. Today was for looking forward, not for looking back, and then she was most decidedly brought to the present, rudely and painfully, by a man thrusting his way through the crowded pavement.

'Well, really! Some people!' she expostulated, rubbing her bruised shoulder and turning to glare at the offending back of the man who was now rapidly disappearing from view.

'Couldn't care tuppence about anybody else,' grumbled a fellow sufferer, busily rescuing the contents of her shopping bag from between people's legs. Frances bent to help her, reaching for an errant apple that had rolled further than the rest, and when all were retrieved the lady shopper thanked her and hurried on her way, still muttering her grievances.

Frances was about to follow when something made her hesitate. The lone apple had rolled to the feet of someone looking in a nearby window, and although Frances had at first assumed that this someone was window-shopping, she now had second thoughts. The lady, who was elderly, had not moved and was leaning against the glass in a manner which caused Frances to walk over and say cautiously :

'Excuse me, are you all right?' A closer look made her add urgently : 'Here, lean on me. You're not well, are you? Shall I get help?'

Although in distress, the woman said with great dignity :

'My dear, if you could oblige me ...' and she indicated a brown leather handbag on her arm. 'A pill box ... in the zipper compartment.' The words, in a pleasant, cultured voice, were haltingly spoken.

Frances quickly did as she was bidden, found the box and extracted a white tablet which she handed over. Her companion shakily placed it on her tongue and for a few moments they remained standing quietly, Frances still half supporting her.

She ought to have medical attention, Frances thought uneasily, casting her eyes along Regent Street for a passing taxi. There were, as usual, plenty about, but to her exasperation all were taken.

'Don't worry, my dear, I am quite used to this and shall be better in a moment when the tablet has had time to take effect,' her companion murmured, sensing her agitation.

Frances thought otherwise and thankfully now caught sight of an empty cab cruising towards them. She waved an imperious arm and to her relief it pulled in to the kerb.

'Here's a taxi now,' she said calmly. 'Come along ... take your time and lean on me.'

'It's very kind of ...'

'Don't talk. I'm sure it would be better not to,' Frances cut in swiftly. 'We'll soon have you safely home.'

The driver had now left his seat to help and together they managed to manoeuvre the stricken woman into the back of the taxi.

'She isn't going to pass out, is she?' he asked anxiously, looking at the ashen face of his passenger as she lay back against the upholstered seat, and Frances replied:

'I don't know ... you'd better get a move on,' and to her companion she added as she joined her: 'Where shall I say?'

Indecision passed over the other's face. An independent lady, Frances thought with some sympathy, and solved the matter by announcing firmly: 'I shall come with you and make sure you reach home safely. Now, where shall I tell the driver to take us?'

An address was given and before closing once more, a pair of shrewd eyes made a probing appraisal.

Frances remained silent, eyeing the woman with interest. From the top of her beautifully groomed white hair to the tips of her tiny grey buttoned boots, she bespoke gentility and prosperity, unobtrusive but unmistakably one of the aristocracy. Her age was hard to define—the rather autocratic face was drawn with lines of pain and suffering—but Frances ventured a guess at around the seventy mark. Not for her was there a falling of standards with the years, and Frances somehow knew that she would always be particular of how she looked and dressed. The double row of pearls and the fur coat she was wearing, even to Frances' inexperienced eye, looked real, and the stones in her rings certainly had not come out of a Christmas cracker!

A movement of the hand bearing these rings, rigidly clutching the handle of her cane, caused Frances to look up to find her companion's eyes disconcertingly upon her.

'How do you feel now?' she asked anxiously.

'Very much better. Please, don't look so worried, my dear. You have been a tremendous help to me—not many would have been so kind to a stranger. I do hope I am not inconveniencing you in any way?' Her voice was almost pedantic in the way of speech, but had great charm.

'Not at all,' Frances hastily assured her, refusing to sneak a look at her watch, and mentally kissing the audition goodbye. 'Will there be someone in when we get you home?' she added, and relaxed when this was confirmed.

The taxi swung round a corner and began to slow down, and looking out of the window Frances gave an inward smile, thinking how well her lady fitted into the respectable surroundings of the prosperous square they had just entered. The age of gracious living was rapidly disappearing—many of the fine old houses in London being converted into offices and flats—and so it was with a keen interest that she eyed the elegant Georgian architecture that met her eyes.

When the cab stopped she opened her door and ran quickly up the four stone steps, pressing her finger on the bell and keeping it there, proclaiming urgency. When the door opened a manservant appeared, his questioning look altering as his eyes moved past her, taking in the scene. With an exclamation of alarm he hurried past her, Frances at his heels, relieved that the burden of responsibility was being taken from her.

By this time the driver had once more alighted and between them the two men assisted the sick woman into the house. Frances hovered uncertainly on the pavement, giving a quick glance at her watch, and when the driver reappeared, she shot into the cab and waited with growing impatience until he slid back into his seat. Leaning forward, she said briskly:

'Edgware Road, please—the television studios—and I'm late.'

'Right you are, miss!' The driver swung the cab away and accelerated rapidly. 'A pleasure dealing with toffs like that,' he announced, nodding in the direction of the house. 'They know how to treat you right.'

Obviously well tipped, thought Frances with amusement, glancing out of the window for another look as they circled the well-kept grass that made the centrepiece of the Square. She wished she had had the chance to say goodbye. As the cab swung towards the exit of the Square Frances caught sight of the manservant emerging from the house, standing looking after them, and then the cab turned the corner and the scene was lost from view.

She gave her watch another look, resignation finally setting in. Auditions and casting directors wait for no man, she thought philosophically, but what else could she have done, under the circumstances? Leave the poor woman to collapse in the middle of Regent Street? Zoe would naturally understand, and agree with the outcome, but she would also point out that these sort of things were always happening to Frances—that she attracted people in trouble and stray dogs like honey to the bee!

'Here we are, miss.' The driver turned and looked at her with interest. 'Are you on the telly, then? Don't rightly know that I recognise you ...' and he paused expectantly.

'No, I don't suppose you do,' Frances told him, getting out her purse and gloomily doubting future prospects.

'The other party paid for the cab-fare,' he answered cheerfully.

That's good news, she thought, watching him drive away before making towards the entrance to the studios. Running her eyes down the notice board displayed inside she found the name she wanted—Deverell, room four, eighth floor.

Two girls and a lone man were already waiting for the lift, the girls talking in low tones, the man, shoulders hunched, hands in pockets, staring intently down at his feet. With a hiss the lift doors opened and as its passengers emerged, the four stepped in to take their place. The girls left at the fourth floor and the man paused, finger poised, and Frances came out of her reverie and said quickly:

'Oh! Sorry—eighth, please,' and he pressed the appropriate button without a word and the doors closed and the lift began to ascend again. Apart from giving her a cursory look, the man took no further interest in her, but remained staring down, arms folded across his chest, a frown on his face.

Someone else with troubles, Frances thought with an inward sigh. How come on a day as important as today everything seemed to be against her? Even the floor number! Eight! Why couldn't it have been two, or even five? she argued silently, and raised her eyes to the indicator light, impatiently watching it click from the fifth, sixth, and seventh floors. She again glanced at her watch and stifled a groan. What was she bothering to go for?

The lift stopped and she waited for the doors to open, taking a step forward in anticipation. The man at her side also straightened and together they waited expectantly. Almost in unison their eyes moved upwards to the indicator light which had stopped ominously between number seven and eight.

'Oh, no!' exclaimed Frances, thinking despairingly

that this was the last straw! She looked across in consternation at her companion who was now contemplating the list of emergency instructions attached to the wall panel, a resigned look on his face. Frances glared back at the indicator light, willing it to move.

'Are we stuck?' she asked, knowing it was a stupid question but needing something to say. He swung his head round and stared, his look of impatience changing slightly. Good, she thought, at least he's acknowledging my existence. She was beginning to think that perhaps she had become invisible!

The stare bordered almost on rudeness and Frances would have been annoyed except that she could have been accused of the same bad manners. For she found herself gazing into the most amazing eyes she had ever encountered. Yellow-brown eyes, topaz eyes ... cool, speculative cat's eyes.

He broke the silence between them by saying laconically: 'We are,' reaching out to press the alarm bell, and then returning to his leaning position with a calmness that should have been reassuring but which, in fact, was rather irritating.

'Does it do this very often?' she enquired, and jabbing at the alarm bell again, this time keeping his finger there for some seconds, he replied:

'Not that I am aware of.'

Silence once more and Frances eased her weight from one foot to the other, her annoyance growing. She didn't expect specialist treatment, but on the other hand it would be nice to share a joking camaraderie about their situation, which after all was not a particularly pleasant one. Instead of which her companion-in-misfortune looked as though he was afraid she was about to ask him for a loan! If she didn't get a job soon, she thought grimly, she might be reduced to doing just that, but not from toffee-nose over there! If he considered his aloof expression and controlled patience to her questions a way of snubbing her, then he was sadly mistaken. How did he know that she didn't suffer from galloping claustrophobia? she asked herself indignantly. It would serve him right if she went into hysterics! She gave a heavy sigh, hoping to attract his attention, until another thought struck her. She slanted him a look. He seemed normal, but many a maniac was hidden behind an unremarkable exterior. Right on cue his dry voice cut into her rapidly growing imagination.

'Don't look so worried. You'll have to take my word for it that I'm not an escaped rapist.'

'That's nice to know,' she answered crossly, annoyed that her thoughts should have been read so accurately. She sighed audibly. 'They must be aware outside that we've stopped, surely?'

He shrugged. 'I suggest you put all your faith in the alarm.'

In other words, shut up.

It would serve him right if she fainted at his feet, she thought, glumly coming to the conclusion that he would probably leave her right where she fell. Or she might even start to take all her clothes off in a panic, that would show him! and she stifled a giggle—it would, indeed! She cast her eyes round the walls of their small cell and finding nothing of interest to occupy her, decided it would be more interesting to study the other occupant.

Had she called him normal? That had been a mistake. There was nothing normal or unremarkable about this man. Middle thirties, she guessed, with a determined, rather haughty face—all sharp lines and angles—although there was indication that he smiled sometimes in the tiny wrinkles at the corner of his eyes and the deep clefts running from nose to jaw. The nose was straight and the jaw a no-nonsense one. His dark brown hair grew from a peak above a brooding forehead and that tan had never been achieved in England, certainly not on last summer's quota of sun! The sweater and slacks, although casual, had the aura of Knightsbridge all over them and though not overtly muscular, he looked as though he could be useful with a squash racquet in his hand or track shoes on his feet. He also had a very pleasing voice, what little she had heard of it, and this, coupled with the sight of a folded script peeping out from his back pocket, pointed to him being an actor.

An intriguing specimen, Frances mused, but it was the eyes that really held. Although they had only been cast her way briefly she wanted to see if they were really flecked with yellow, or whether the peculiar lighting in the lift had changed ordinary hazel into something more unusual.

She had her wish, for at that moment the thickly lashed lids were lifted to reveal a cool regard. Their impact was as strong as she expected, but he didn't speak and she was aware of a stupid feeling of disappointment. Perhaps he doesn't like women? she thought, as quickly rejecting the idea. There had been something in that look that told her he was all man, and as no woman likes to be totally ignored, and Frances always had had an impish sense of humour, some devil prompted her to say, her voice faltering and full of apprehension:

'H ... how long will the oxygen hold out, do you think?'

She might have guessed that he wasn't easily fooled ... but at least he was rewarding her with his full attention. With raised brows his eyes lifted expressively to the ventilation shaft above their heads and then back again to her face.

'You're not going to become hysterical, I hope?' he asked, in a voice that spoke volumes. Woe betide hysterical women!

'No, I'm not,' Frances replied with great charm, 'at

least, I don't think I am, but I'm not making any promises. It all depends upon how long we're in this delightful situation.' She changed her weight on to the other foot, wedging herself more comfortably into the corner. 'Do I look the hysterical type?' she added curiously.

He gave her a long critical inspection. Frances was well used to being looked over by prospective theatrical managements, but suddenly, to her intense disgust and surprise, she found herself blushing deeply as his eyes travelled lazily over her, a gleam of amusement lurking in the back of the openly shameless regard. Too late to retract, Frances lifted her chin, a small smile of defiance playing on her lips, cursing her stupidity and knowing what he could see ...

A female who talked too much, middle twenties, height five seven, figure nicely rounded, what was visible. Wearing shaggy simulated fur jacket and heavy brown wool skirt, mid-calf. Neat feet clad in tan suede knee-length boots. Good deportment when not slouched against wall. So much for the body—now for the head. Rather a roundish face, good skin, fair with a generous natural colour and a hint of freckles over the bridge of a nondescript nose. Full, bow-shaped mouth, wide smile, good teeth, friendly blue eyes and attractive voice. Hair— well, that was to remain a mystery. Pulled down securely against the keen wind, over a wide, intelligent brow, was a thickly knitted cloche hat, the green matching her ribbed jumper.

Frances mourned the hat. It hid, according to her, the only asset she possessed ... she could be grateful to the gods for her thick abundance of hair, but she had no intention of letting this lecherous moron opposite in on the act!

'Well?' she prompted sweetly, every nerve telling her that although this man might not be a maniac he was certainly dangerous, acknowledging his attraction, while hackles rose against the bold, cynical appraisal which she was sure was supposed to teach her a lesson. Against what? she thought indignantly. Talking to strangers in lifts, or only him in particular?

He waved a hand expressively. 'One can never tell. I suspect you're more choleric than hysterical, but I do hope you keep on the optimistic side ... I don't like slapping females.'

Not only dangerous, but also a liar, fumed Frances inwardly. He was the epitome of egotistical male happily slapping down any female who stepped out of line. She could almost hear the whip cracking!

'I'm very glad to hear it,' she ground out, smiling through her teeth. 'And as for being choleric ...' and she stopped, finding a disconcerting gleam at the back of the tawny eyes and realising that her sense of humour was being paid back in kind. 'Very funny,' she said sarcastically, and marched the few paces to the control panel to press all floor buttons, one by one, in varying combinations, her finger stabbing with full force. Nothing happened, and glancing impatiently at her watch she resumed her initial position, refusing to meet his eyes.

It was not in her nature to remain on her dignity for long, however, and looking across the space between them, she asked: 'Do you think it would be any use shouting?'

'I doubt it,' the superior being replied, and following her gaze to the small trap in the roof, he added sardonically: 'And I have no intention of doing a James Bond either.'

'No one's asking you to,' Frances replied kindly, thereby implying that she quite realised he wasn't up to it but that she understood and forgave. His lips twitched and her spirits lifted. He wasn't such a stuffed shirt after all. Since she was a friendly, gregarious soul, uncommunicative, inscrutable men bugged her, but the twitching lips was a point in his favour. She chose to forget the bold look and high-handed manner for the sake of sanity.

She eased her weight once again, saying: 'I think I'll sit down. I didn't have anything to eat at lunch-time and all this standing is beginning to tell,' and pulling a newspaper out of her bag she spread it on the floor in her corner and settled herself down. Her eyes began to idly scan that part of the paper not covered by herself and her interest quickened. She leaned forward, finger to print.

' "Let the Stars Foretell!" ' she read out portentously, and then looked up, eyes alight. 'I don't believe in horoscopes, but they can be entertaining. At least, there might be something in birth signs. I once had a job as a typist to a woman astrologer—she was writing a book about reading the stars and recognising people born under the different signs of the Zodiac. Quite a bit rubbed off and stuck.'

'Really?'

'Yes . . . it's rather complicated actually. Did you know that the sun changes signs not on the stroke of midnight, which would be awfully convenient, wouldn't it, but at variable times during the day. That's why to obtain an accurate chart you have to give the time of your birth as well as the day and year, and even then it depends on other planets ascending or descending. I'm not sure which.' She grinned at her vagueness and returned to the printed page, eyes swiftly passing down the column. 'Listen to this for Libra—that's me. "Favourable aspects lie ahead, especially financial ones. Be wary of hasty judgments, patience will be rewarded. Red is the colour for this week." ' She slanted him a look, pulling a face. 'I can do with a favourable financial aspect and can be patient if necessary, but the colour is right out. I never wear red. So that's that.' She tilted her head consideringly, a teasing look on her face. 'Do you want to know your forecast?' she asked.

'I'd rather make my own destiny, thank you,' her companion drawled, jabbing again at the alarm button as he spoke.

'Ah! a definite non-believer,' murmured Frances. 'If I knew you better I might have a stab at a guess.'

'Who knows, you might get the chance; if we're in here much longer we'll be reduced to telling our life histories,' he remarked dryly.

'I have the feeling that it would be me who did all the talking,' Frances answered, equally dry. 'You're not a communicative person, are you? Mmm ... that should give me a clue!' and she leaned her head against the wall and contemplated him, eyes half-closed, '... so that rules out Leo, and Aries. Taurus or possibly Virgo?' she asked tentatively, and seeing his face knew she had failed and gave a laugh. 'Oh, well, it's all a load of rubbish. You can twist anything to fit it if you really want to. And folk always preen themselves for the good bits and deny that they're anything like the bad!'

She rose to her feet, folding up the paper and giving an involuntary yawn. 'Oh, dear ... how long have we been in here now?'

'Twenty minutes.'

'Is that all? Ye gods, it seems like twenty hours!' She paused from brushing down her skirt to grimace. 'Sorry, didn't mean to sound so rude, but ...' She pursed her lips thoughtfully. 'How about Cancer ...?' and then was flung violently off balance as the lift jolted into life, descending at an alarming rate.

When it finally came to an abrupt halt somewhere between floors three and four, Frances found her face buried in lambswool, the stranger's arms tightly round her. They had collapsed into a heap on the floor after he had tried to save her fall, only to overbalance himself.

She couldn't have moved at that moment even if her stomach had allowed her. She had left it up there between seven and eight and it was taking a little time to catch up, or rather down, and the lift, although now stationary, seemed to be whizzing round and round.

It didn't matter, however. The arms were strong and comforting and the sweater beneath her cheek soft. She could hear his heart beating with reassuring regularity and with an amazing rush of surprise Frances realised just how long it had been since she lay in a man's arms. Getting over Mark and trying to forget Chichester and her last love affair had taken time.

Pushing herself up with as much dignity as she could muster, she at last breathed: 'Sorry, I ...' but her legs would not obey her head—that errant stomach had now come winging home, and a wave of nausea swept over her.

'It's a good job I learned to play Rugby football,' he said, sitting upright and holding her steady.

'If it does that again I shall be sick,' she managed.

'Not over me, I hope,' came the dry rejoinder, as he rose to his feet bringing her with him, and then: 'Hold tight, here we go again,' and this time they shot upwards.

With a jolt that caused them both to stagger, the lift stopped, and the doors opened with as much aplomb as if they had been behaving perfectly all day. Without a pause Frances was hauled bodily out into the corridor where there was an immediate babble of excited voices. She opened her eyes and as quickly shut them. It was better to feel everything going round rather than to actually see it doing so. Over and above everything else came the voice of her companion, curt and decisive.

'Put that chair between the doors to stop them closing, will you, please? and you—telephone down to Maintenance ... open that window and bring another chair,' and the arms, those nicely comforting arms, led

her staggeringly along for a few yards, pressured her
into sitting down and then were taken away.

Beautiful fresh air ...

With eyes still closed Frances lay back, aware of things
going on around her, but not caring. After a short while
she heard someone come over to her.

'Breathe in deeply,' a voice ordered, and then : 'There's
no need to wait, thank you. She'll be all right,' and footsteps receded, accompanied by subdued talk, and gradually everything quietened.

'I daren't be anything else,' she murmured, testing her
eyes carefully and finding her lift companion staring
down at her, 'or else you'd probably toss me down the
lift shaft!' She grimaced and put a hand to her head.
'How do you know I'm all right?'

'Because the colour is coming back to your cheeks,'
came the equable reply.

'It isn't good for anyone to be so sure of himself,' she
retorted.

There was a touch of amusement in his voice. 'You did
very well back there. I didn't think for one moment that
you would panic, but you can never be sure how people
will react.'

'Well, thank you very much! You might have given
some indication of what you felt! But then, as we've
already agreed, you're not the communicative type. And
I think that I should add that I'm not usually so talka-
tive.'

He smiled. 'I'm sure you're not.'

'Yes, well ...' Frances looked away. That smile, when
genuine, was really something. The lift doors gaped invitingly, only the chair looked incongruous, half in, half
out. Turning back, she continued politely : 'Please don't
let me delay you any longer.'

'I'm in no hurry. Who have you come to see?'

'I'm supposed to see a Mr Deverell—Tom Deverell.' She

shrugged. 'I was late anyway. Do you know him?' Suddenly arrested by the look on his face, she stared. 'You're not him, are you?'

He gave a slightly malicious smile. 'That would be the final straw, wouldn't it? No, I'm not, but I was on my way to join him.'

'You were? How extraordinary.' Frances felt relief sweep over her. For some reason the thought of depending on this man for a job was faintly alarming.

'So you're an actress, are you? I thought you said you were a typist?'

'Only when I'm out of work,' she explained.

'I see.' He closed the window, remarking casually: 'I thought Tom had finished all the auditions.'

'I'm sure he has,' Frances agreed, standing up carefully. 'Do you think it's worth searching for him?'

'Why not? And in view of the fact that you've had no lunch, we should search for a hot drink,' he replied shortly. 'Come along. Girls who diet want their heads examining.'

'I'm not dieting,' protested Frances. 'I can never eat before an audition—I'm too nervous!'

'No doubt fainting at the director's feet has its possibilities,' he said impatiently, drawing her along the corridor. 'We're on the seventh so we have to walk a flight.' He stopped. 'Unless you want to use the other lift?'

'Ha, ha,' she commented dourly as they moved towards the stairs, and he gave a brief smile. They climbed for a few seconds in silence and then he asked:

'Do you always turn up late for auditions?'

'No, I do not!' The question, although a legitimate one, rankled. It was no business of his. 'I have an adequate and quite truthful explanation for Mr Deverell, should he be willing to listen to it.'

'Oh, I expect he will, if you smile at him nicely. He won't mind if it's truthful or not.'

Frances was the one to stop now. 'It's a good job you're not Tom Deverell, isn't it? It's quite obvious that my smile wouldn't work with you!' She sighed heavily, took a deep breath and tried again, her voice all reasonableness. 'Look, you've probably had one hell of a day where nothing's gone right for you, but please, don't take it out on me. This audition happens to be important to me and I've probably fouled it up through no fault of my own. Do you think you could find this man Deverell and then you can wash your hands of me and go your own sweet way. In the meantime, I shall be practising my smile.' She challenged him with her eyes and he replied blandly :

'Yes, I think I can do that for you, though you may have to wait while I find him.' They had come to a halt outside a door. He pushed it open and ushered her in, the latch clicking loudly behind her.

Frances took in the room with one critical sweeping glance. It looked familiar, like all abandoned rehearsal rooms. A forlorn feeling swept over her and she wandered disconsolately to a chair and sat down, her eyes passing from the table, still untidy with papers and filled ashtrays, to the piano and a number of chairs scattered about in the otherwise empty room. It was no use. The auditions were over and done with. Why was she waiting? She might just as well go home.

The door opened and a girl came in, carrying a cup.

'There's sugar in the saucer, if you want it,' she said kindly, without preamble. 'Felix said even if you don't usually take it, you're to do so now, but then Felix likes giving his orders,' and before Frances could say anything more than a surprised 'thank you' the girl hurried out.

Felix ...

Frances sipped the coffee gratefully, wondering at his thoughtfulness. The name suited him. She shrugged ... more than likely she would never see him again and he would become merely 'the man in the lift' in her memory ... but she thanked him for the coffee. Draining the last dregs she placed the cup carefully on the table and tried to relax.

And waited ...

CHAPTER TWO

'HERE we are! Well now, Felix has explained all about the delay,' a cheery voice said from the open doorway, and Frances looked up to see a stockily built man of middle years come bustling towards her. 'Bad luck being stuck like that ... nasty experience ... must have been most upsetting. Good job you had Felix to look after you ... very dependable,' and he held out his hand, a wide smile on his face.

Frances hastily stood up and offered her own. 'Mr Deverell?' she asked.

'That's right ... now I suggest you take a script and read the section marked ...'

'You want me to audition?' stammered Frances, hardly able to believe her good fortune.

'Are you fit enough now, or would you like to come back tomorrow?' Tom Deverell was fumbling around on the desk until he found the script. 'It would be easier now, of course. Lifts ... I hate them, but in a building this size they're a necessity. Hope you're not going to sue us!' and he beamed up at her.

Frances warmed to this friendly man and smiled. 'No, I don't think I'll be doing that.'

'Good, good. How do you feel, then? Willing and able?'

'Yes, I'll be glad to audition.' Frances nearly laughed at the inadequacy of her reply.

Deverell glanced over to the door. 'Ah, Felix, there you are. I think we've time to audition Miss ... er ... I'm afraid I don't know your name ...'

'Heron. Frances Heron,' supplied Frances. 'I have a list of my past experience here,' and she rummaged in her bag and brought out a foolscap sheet of paper, wondering as she did so why this Felix person should be in on things ... *him* she could do without! Her eyes flickered in his direction and whatever thoughts were on his mind seemed as though they were disagreeable ones, by the forbidding look on his face.

'Splendid! You go over there and read the passages while I glance at the list,' Tom Deverell suggested, and Frances moved to the chair he indicated. She managed to read the pieces through three times before he bounced to his feet, saying: 'Ready when you are, Miss Heron.' He crossed to her. 'As you've probably gathered, the story is set in Cornwall in the early eighteen hundreds. I suppose it could be termed an historical romance—it includes the politics of the time, life in the grand house as opposed to a fisherman's cottage, smuggling, storms at sea, all the ingredients that go to make a good serial— at least, so we hope!' He enjoyed his own joke for a few seconds and then went on: 'The hero is a fellow called Nick Penruth—*Penruth* being the title of the serial. As you see, the part you're reading is that of Mary Trewith. It's all shades of *Lorna Doone*,' he added, beaming enthusiastically.

'Doone country is in Devon, Tom,' came the dry voice from behind. 'Shades of *Jamaica Inn*, perhaps?'

'Yes, well, it's all the same,' Deverell said blithely.

Not to a Cornishman, thought Frances, and she could tell that the man Felix thought the same and gave him a small smile which he ignored.

'Right, Miss Heron, if you're ready?' Deverell asked. Frances nodded and swung off the fur jacket, throwing it carelessly across the back of the chair. She then pulled off the cloche hat and shook her head, freeing the mass of chestnut hair, running her fingers carelessly through the waves. She turned to the two men ready for further instructions and then waited uncertainly. The man Felix wore his usual enigmatic face, but Deverell's was alive with delight and he rubbed his hands together gleefully.

'Well, well, this is something more like! My word, yes!' He stopped and added anxiously: 'You do have a Cornish accent in your repertoire, don't you, Miss Heron?' and sighed with relief on her nod of assent. 'Then let's get started.'

'Tom has asked me to read Penruth. I hope you have no objections, Miss Heron?' the man Felix murmured, leading her to the centre of the room while Deverell hurried back to the table and seated himself.

'None whatsoever,' replied Frances coolly, trying to kid both of them, not at all happy about the way her surmise that he was an actor had been proven. She made a conscious effort to relax and hoped he wouldn't see the script trembling in her hand.

'You may have gathered from Tom's preamble that Penruth is gentry and Mary local girl. This first scene follows on from where she has saved Penruth's life by rowing out to rescue him from rocks after his boat has been smashed up by a storm. The second scene is after he has married Mary and is confronting her in a jealous rage for a supposed indiscretion on her part. This is a fiery quarrel ending in a passionate embrace.' His voice was strictly impersonal and the tawny eyes were half hidden by dropped lids. 'Ready?'

Frances nodded. Afterwards, she had to admit that her co-actor gave her as much help as it was possible to give, feeding her the lines beautifully. Yes, she would hand that to him—he could act, and this quite naturally brought up her own performance, her voice with the

Cornish burr contrasting nicely with his rather attractive one.

And could the fact that Deverell asked them to do the quarrel scene twice be something in her favour? She hoped so. Admittedly, it was difficult to struggle with someone holding a script and reading from it, and it would be safe to assume that the second time round would be better. It was—not for that reason, but because her co-actor took every advantage of the kiss allowed him in the script. Finally pulling herself away, eyes sparkling with anger, she spoke the ensuing lines with personal fervour and wished she could do the face-slapping bit that followed in the story.

He had known exactly how she was feeling, saying with a gleam of amusement in his eyes: 'We cut here, Miss Heron. A shame for you, but you can't expect an actor to be slapped consistently throughout an afternoon of auditions.' He smiled, enjoying her discomposure. 'I'm sure you can slap beautifully, just as you anger beautifully.' He then turned, saying casually: 'Sufficient, Tom?'

'Thank you, Felix, yes. Will you come over here and join me, Miss Heron?' Deverell called, and giving the actor a glacial stare, Frances stalked over to the desk, head held high, every proud bone in her body showing just what she thought of him.

Deverell looked up and smiled encouragingly. 'Thank you. Your reading was most interesting. Do sit down. From this list I see you've played Bristol, Queensbridge, Rotheringham, Leicester and Chichester ...'

'Yes, I've only listed the roles worthy of any note,' agreed Frances. She could see the man Felix out of the corner of her eye, sitting a few yards away, legs out-stretched, contemplating the tip of his highly polished shoes.

'You had good reviews at Chichester,' continued Deverell, and she nodded.

'I was lucky with my director and co-actors.'

'You haven't done television work before, but that's not too important ... and you've done period costume.' There was silence while he carried on reading the list, his thumb tapping the paper thoughtfully. This pause was broken by a slow voice from the other chair.

'Acting for television is a totally different technique from the live theatre. Does Miss Heron realise that?'

The two men looked at her consideringly and Deverell raised his brows at her questioningly.

'Yes, I do, but I'm sure I could pick up the technique quickly—I presume your director is capable of teaching me?' Frances answered evenly, referring the words to Deverell but meaning them for long-legs over there. She was rewarded by a bark of laughter from the casting director and a slight change of position from long-legs.

'Yes, I think he is,' agreed Deverell, still highly amused. 'I like your accent, Miss Heron. It sounds native, is it?'

'No. I spent my early childhood years there.'

'Ah, that accounts for it ... yes, the accent comes over most natural.' He rubbed his chin thoughtfully. 'That's all, I think. We'll be in touch—we do have your address, don't we?' Deverell rose with a smile and walked round the table, fetching her coat and helping her on with it. 'You should hear one way or the other in about five days.' He held out his hand and shook hers firmly. 'Glad you didn't miss the audition ... and I apologise again on behalf of our lift! You can find your own way out, can't you?' and when she smiled and nodded, he then threw a: 'Won't be a minute, Felix, wait for me, will you?' over his shoulder and giving Frances a friendly nod, Deverell left the room.

Frances took her time getting ready to go. She wasn't going to let Felix whoever-he-was fluster her. She twisted her hair into a knot before pulling on the cloche, tucking in some stray wisps at the back that had escaped. She collected her bag and finally looked across the room. He was now tilting his chair backwards, balancing it on two legs, watching her with disconcerting intensity, hands behind his head.

'I was right about the choleric, wasn't I?' he drawled. 'Temper and red hair always go together.'

Red hair! He'd said that on purpose. Her hair was truly deep chestnut, like the colour of a highly polished conker. She smiled pityingly.

'Do you know, I've heard that said so often I might come to believe it in time!' She thrust her bag beneath her arm and hesitated, saying stiffly: 'Thank you for the coffee, it was a life-saver.'

He inclined his head and sketched a salute, his face as polite as her own, only his eyes challenging her politeness.

Halfway to the door she turned. 'I think your birthday's in November—and if it isn't, it ought to be! You're a classic arrogant Scorpio!' and rounding on her heel she swept out.

As she marched along the corridor Frances made a fervent wish that the chair would overbalance and send him crashing to the floor—but it wouldn't, it never did, to cocksure people like that. More's the pity!

'I think you're in with a good chance,' said Zoe. She was painting her fingernails a bright scarlet, the tip of her tongue peeping between lips of the same colour as an aid to concentration. 'From what you tell me, you gave a good reading. Tom Deverell was taken with your physical appearance and liked your accent.'

Frances looked up from the book she was reading and shook her head, asking: 'Do you know him? Was he your "influential source"?'

'No—I heard from a friend of a friend, you know the way it is.' Frowning slightly, Zoe inspected her handiwork, then considered her friend, brush poised. 'It was funny you getting stuck in that lift, Frankie.'

'Hilarious!'

'Typical, of course.'

'What do you mean? I've never been stuck in a lift before in my life!' responded Frances indignantly. 'And I don't ever want to be again.'

'What about the old lady who was ill? Just you! Still, you couldn't leave her, and everything turned out okay in the end,' Zoe continued, impervious to the indignation. 'I think that actor put a good word in for you with Deverell.' She waved her hands in the air to dry the polish. 'You say he was good in the part of Penruth?'

'Uhuh ... very,' replied Frances, her nose in the book again. She had said very little to Zoe about the man Felix, but despite this he still kept coming into the conversation. Had he put in a word for her? she wondered. He had been uncommunicative in the lift, but not hostile. Only later, at the audition, had she sensed an indefinable something, almost antipathy, in his cool scrutiny. Her thoughts were broken by Zoe, who said:

'I can't think of any actor called Felix, can you? Of course, he may be basically a television actor and we hardly ever get the chance to view, treading the boards nightly as we do. That's something, Frankie—if you do get the part you'll be working during the day with lots of lovely free evenings.' She screwed the top on to the nail varnish bottle and began to clear the table. 'We'll just have to cross our fingers and wait. It's about time something good happened to you. Since Chichester your shining talent has been somewhat hidden beneath ghastly comedies or equally ghastly whodunits!'

Frances laughed at the dour note in her voice. 'You can't blame management when those sort of plays do good-box office,' she argued reasonably, 'and it's a job with a pay-packet at the end of it. As for Chichester— well, that's another story, isn't it?'

'Are you completely over Mark now, Frankie?' Zoe asked quietly.

Frances pondered the question, staring pensively out of the window, thinking about Mark Lucas.

'Don't bother to answer if I'm stepping where angels fear to tread,' added Zoe during the pause.

'I don't mind, Zoe. It's all over—has been for weeks now. Six months is a long time for a heart to heal that wasn't really broken in the first place.'

'Thank goodness for that,' breathed Zoe. 'I haven't probed because I know what it's like, but honestly, Frankie love, you're better out of it.'

'I know,' murmured Frances, rubbing her fingers against the pile on one of the velvet cushions. 'I knew then, but knowing and doing are two different things, aren't they? There was no choice but for me to cut and run, not when I managed to think coherently, but the effort at the time was painful.' She shrugged. 'From now on I'm off men! I'm going to concentrate on my career.'

Zoe gave an amused cackle. 'Now I've heard everything! You may want to be "little sister" to them, but you'll not be allowed the part! And you're not made to be a spinster, kiddo. Your trouble is that you draw the little-boy-lost types like a magnet, and they're not your sort.'

'Really? And what is my sort?' Frances asked dryly.

'What you really need is a strong, dominant male. Someone who can match you in an argument and who has the sense to stop you taking over. I've told you time and time again, Frankie, that men don't like women being more capable than themselves. It positively shrivels that tiny seed of love worse than a drought! I know you've had to stand on your own two feet for so long that you've had to be independent, but you must learn to play it down.' Zoe was really warming to her theme now, and hitched her chair closer. 'You need a man who makes instant decisions, the right ones, of course, and who'll encourage you to be the little woman now and again. A man as intelligent as yourself who you can respect and lean on.'

'And just where does this paragon exist?' asked Frances mildly.

'He exists, kiddo, make no mistake. Just be sure he isn't an actor!'

'They're the only men I meet,' offered Frances, 'and I loathe dominant men, they always rub me up the wrong way. Anyway, I thought you were anti-falling in love? Aren't your aims on a higher, mercenary level?'

Zoe grinned wickedly. 'I could marry for money, but I doubt you can, and I don't particularly want you to fall in love—only six months is a long time for a young and healthy heart to remain in cold storage. There's a danger you'll lose it to someone totally unsuitable again.'

'Mark wasn't unsuitable exactly ...'

'No, only married.' Zoe raised her eyes in wonderment. 'He was a dimwit if he hadn't found out about your puritan streak before offering you his all.' She stood up. 'Coffee?' and at Frances' smile of agreement, she disappeared into the kitchen.

Dear Zoe, Frances thought with affection. She put down her book and thought back to that first meeting with Zoe at drama school, six years ago, and how she had been immediately attracted to the tall, leggy brunette, Zoe Aleksander. She was a couple of years older than Frances, with her own brand of drawling wit, and the attraction had been reciprocated. Zoe had taken the younger girl under her wing, inviting her back to her parents' home as soon as she found out how alone in the world Frances was. The Aleksanders knew all about being alone and friendless, having fled the horrors of Warsaw and sought refuge in England. They were a charming couple and Frances loved them dearly.

'Mama rang tonight,' Zoe declared, coming in with the coffee. 'I told her about your audition and she says she can't wait until she's watching you on the box.'

'If I get the job! She's rather premature,' protested Frances.

'You sound unduly pessimistic considering how well the audition seems to have gone. Is there something you're keeping to yourself that I should know?' Zoe demanded, handing over a mug, frowning as she changed her line of thought. 'This Felix person, I'm sure I ought to be able to place him. What's he like? Attractive?'

'That all depends on what you mean by ...'

'Yes, yes, I know! but even if the man doesn't appeal to you personally, do you reckon he has sex appeal, for goodness' sake!'

Frances laughed at Zoe's exasperation. 'Yes, he has sex appeal,' she admitted, seeing the tall, lean figure in her mind's eye, leaning against the lift wall contemplating her. 'He's tallish, darkish, good-looking in an angular sort of way, and I imagine he has no difficulty in finding a bedmate. There, does that satisfy you?'

'I bet it satisfies him,' drawled Zoe, eyeing her friend with interested eyes. 'But does he appeal to you?' she persisted, and Frances returned the look, measure for measure, and then gave in, her face breaking into a reluctant grin.

'Yes, Zoe, to my annoyance, but the feeling isn't reciprocated, so you can take that look off your face.'

'How do you know?'

Frances shrugged. 'I overheard something I wasn't meant to hear.'

'Fatal, but irresistible. Go on.'

'I went back for my gloves and the door was open.

Tom Deverell was saying something complimentary about the reading, and he went on about how marvellous my hair would look under the lights. While I was dithering over whether to knock and interrupt them my dear actor friend, in his most cynical voice, said that colour comes out of a bottle these days and not to fall for a pair of blue eyes! He finished off this piece of good advice by saying that I looked like nothing but trouble to him.'

'Male chauvinist pig,' announced Zoe calmly. 'Yet another actor with an inflated ego. We will not become involved emotionally, Frankie, with an actor—let someone else pander to their neuroses.' She stretched out her arms and stifled a yawn, and looking at the clock, exclaimed: 'Heavens—look at the time! I must be off to do my bit.'

'How's the show going?' Frances asked with interest.

'Fine. I can't believe I'm in a West End hit. Eight months and still full houses!'

When Zoe had left for the theatre Frances found her thoughts returning to the television job. She wondered why she felt so upset over the actor's remarks about her and hoped Tom Deverell wouldn't allow himself to be influenced by them. She needed something demanding to go at, something to bring her alive emotionally again. The dreadful ache and deadness that had been with her when she left Chichester was gone and she was beginning to come out of limbo. Spring was having its influence too, and the part of Mary Trewith could prove an exciting challenge, if only she were given the chance to do it. Bother arrogant, enigmatic men and their interfering ways, she grumbled.

She came into contact with that same arrogant, enigmatic man some two weeks later. Right on collision course they met abruptly in the doorway of the Studios and once more his arms grabbed her and her cheek pressed briefly against the hard chest.

'Oh! It's you,' she said shortly, pushing herself away.

'And I might have guessed it would be you,' he answered with heavy calm. 'It does help to look where you're going, you know.'

'Yes, I'm sorry, it was my fault,' she replied, her eyes searching the floor.

'Is this what you're looking for?' he asked, and bent down to retrieve her script. 'I see you've been given the part of Mary Trewith.'

'Yes.' She could have said more, but didn't, and took the script from him. 'I've just collected this.'

'Are you pleased?'

'Of course I'm pleased,' she said, as if talking to an idiot, and then her natural buoyancy bubbled through and she broke into a wide smile. 'Thrilled to bits, actually—and a little scared too. I hope the director will be patient with me at first. Er ... are you playing Nick Penruth?' she asked cautiously, and he gave a sardonic smile.

'No,' and the relief must have shown on her face because he added mockingly : 'More's the pity ... I enjoyed your audition immensely.'

'I wish I could say the same,' Frances replied waspishly, remembering the kiss and feeling her cheeks redden.

'I thought we went rather well together,' he complained in a hurt voice, and Frances gritted her teeth and said what she knew needed to be said.

'Thank you for reading in so well with me, I'm sure that helped.'

'My pleasure,' he replied with exaggeration, 'always ready to oblige ... in any way,' and giving her a knowing smile, he walked on.

Frances resisted the urge to throw something at him—the only thing to hand was the script, and she was going to need that! What is it about that man? she asked herself in exasperation. The minute we start talking like reasonable human beings he drops the acid in. Thank goodness, she thought with fervour, that he's not Penruth! She would have found it difficult to portray love with his mocking eyes looking down at her.

But there was something else. The ridiculous thing was that despite his abrasiveness he made her feel a woman again, and that she found disconcerting. For the past few months her body had been something to be cleaned, dressed and fed. This Felix person somehow brought her alive, proving that there was still red blood coursing through her veins. From someone she didn't even like, the knowledge was humiliating.

Wiping him firmly out of her thoughts, Frances set off to make a return visit to the elegant Georgian house in the Square.

Armed with a bunch of flowers, she pressed her finger to the bell and before she could finish her opening sentence she knew that the manservant had recognised her.

'I've brought the lady of the house some flowers. Would you be kind enough to give them to her for me, please? And perhaps you can tell me if she's feeling better now?'

'Please come in—Lady Ravenscar will be anxious to meet you again,' was the reply, and he stepped back, and after a double blink at the 'Lady Ravenscar' Frances stepped into the hallway.

She was in another era. Everywhere she looked her eyes were held enchanted ... a carved oak chair, a grandfather clock, an exquisite plate on the wall—everything bespoke craftsmanship and loving care. With the warm glow of highly polished wood still with her, Frances entered another room, just as fascinating. It was a long, high-ceilinged room dominated at the far end by a grand piano. Windows were flanked by floor-to-ceiling curtains, the same green repeated throughout, and the whole enhanced by a cream carpet.

Frances recognised Chippendale in the low tables and chairs, and when a china cabinet in the corner caught her eye she wandered over to gaze in admiration at the porcelain displayed behind the glass frontage. She was just running an appreciative eye along the row of bookshelves when the door opened.

Lady Ravenscar, using her cane, walked slowly over to her, a smile of pleasure on her face.

'My dear, how glad I am to see you again! Are these for me? How lovely. Simkin, will you take them away and put them in water, please? Now, my dear, how naughty of you to disappear as you did without allowing me to thank you for your assistance. Do sit down ... thank you, I can manage on this chair quite well.'

Arthritis as well as heart, thought Frances, as she seated herself, and said quickly:

'You're looking much better, I'm so glad. As for dashing away, I'm afraid I was rather short on time. You've been on my conscience ever since and I decided to come and see how you are.'

'I am delighted that you have done so. I have asked Simkin to bring us some tea. I always spoil myself this time in the afternoon. You will stay and join me, won't you?' Lady Ravenscar appealed, and Frances smiled her assent. 'Splendid! Now do take off your coat, my dear, and put it across that chair, you'll be much more comfortable.'

Frances complied and reseated herself, feeling with some amusement rather as though she was being entertained by Royalty. Her hostess's eyes were openly assessing her, but with such unfeigned warmth and kindness that she could not take exception to it.

'How pretty you are, and so young. Well, I don't suppose you think you are young, but from my age ...' She waved a hand impatiently. 'The first thing to do is to introduce ourselves.' She leaned forward, eyes twinkling.

'When I told my family that I had neither your name nor your address they could not believe it! I was cross myself, I can assure you, but we can put that right now,' and she paused, waiting expectantly, and Frances obliged.

'My name is Frances Heron.'

'Frances ... such a lovely name, and one not heard often these days. Mine is Margaret Ravenscar. Ah, here is Simkin with the tea—and the flowers. How beautiful they look in that vase ... I do so love daffodils, don't you? such brave flowers. Thank you, Simkin, you may put them on the piano and we'll have the tea tray on this table, please.' After Simkin had left, Lady Ravenscar beamed with pleasure and asked: 'Frances, will you pour, my dear? I'm not terribly clever at doing such things these days.'

'Yes, of course,' replied Frances, eyeing the fine bone china warily and hoping she wouldn't disgrace herself, but the years of pouring out tea on stage in front of hundreds of eyes held her in good stead and she completed the operation perfectly. 'Do you take sugar, Lady Ravenscar?'

'Thank you, one lump. I *do* enjoy having a visitor—a new face, especially,' Lady Ravenscar told her conspiratorially. 'I am a widow and have been for the past ten years, and although my family visit me as often as their busy lives permit, my life has necessarily been quieter in recent years, owing to my ill health.'

'You are feeling better?'

'I am as well as can be expected, my dear. Although I have learned to live with my ailments sometimes I am a foolish woman. Had you not helped me that day, the consequences, according to my doctor, could have been fatal. I have promised to be good in the future.' She smiled rather sardonically. 'I am not yet ready to leave this world for the next ... there are still some things I have to do,' and with this announcement Lady Ravenscar gestured towards the plate of cakes. 'Do take one, Frances, they are delicious, I can recommend them ... and yes, thank you, I will have another cup of tea,' and she waited in silence while Frances knelt by the tea tray and carefully refilled their cups. 'Now, tell me, what do you do with your life, when you are not rescuing old ladies from their folly?'

'I work in the theatre,' and Frances wondered how this would be accepted. 'I'm an actress,' she further explained.

'How *very* interesting!' Lady Ravenscar's eyes proclaimed this interest and she leaned forward. 'My own family have always had connections with the theatre, in one way or another.' Her eyes twinkled with amusement. 'I had an aunt who made quite a name for herself on the Halls, but she was disowned by the more respectable members of the family, for she took to drink, poor thing. I had aspirations of becoming a concert pianist, and trained until I married ...' Her voice trailed off and for a moment she seemed lost in thought.

'Do you still play?' prompted Frances gently.

Lady Ravenscar followed Frances' gaze towards the piano. 'For my own amusement only, and those times are becoming fewer and fewer. The spirit is eager but the flesh is weak—so depressing. I content myself listening to music.' She waved a hand dismissively. 'So you are an actress ..., what are you doing at the moment?'

'I've just finished a season in repertory theatre and I'm due to begin rehearsing a television series very soon,' Frances replied, hoping that her casualness hid the spurt of pride that accompanied the information.

'Television? Really?' Lady Ravenscar looked gratifyingly impressed. 'My dear girl, ought I to have recognised you?'

Frances laughed and shook her head. 'By no means, this is the first television job I've had.'

'What is it to be? A play?'

'Yes, a serial. What particularly excites me is that it's set in Cornwall, where I lived as a child, and I'm longing to do the location work down there again.'

'More and more interesting. I know Cornwall very well and love it. Are you allowed to tell me what the serial is called?' Lady Ravenscar was watching her with deep interest. 'So that I may be certain to watch it,' she added.

'It's called *Penruth*, but it won't be on for months yet, not until the end of the year probably. They have to plan so far in advance, you know.'

From then on the conversation was decidedly one-sided, as Lady Ravenscar, with gentle probing, was told about the loss of Frances' parents when she was fifteen, right up to the sharing of the apartment with Zoe.

Looking rather anxiously at her hostess, who seemed to be quite flushed, Frances rose to her feet, saying:

'I do hope I haven't tired you, Lady Ravenscar, and overstayed my welcome...?'

Lady Ravenscar shook her head, smiling. 'Not at all, my dear, it has been a most pleasant afternoon, and I hope you will come again. It was kind of you to give me your time.' She hesitated, finger to lip in thought, eyeing her with a speculative gleam. 'I wonder ... it is rather late notice, I know, but I am giving a small dinner party tomorrow evening and I would like you to join us, if you can. Do say you are free.' She looked quickly at her visitor's left hand and raised her brows. 'No ring? No fiancé I should invite to accompany you?' Frances smiled and shook her head and Lady Ravenscar said quickly: 'I cannot think what the young men are doing, a lovely girl like you being allowed to remain unattached! You will come?'

'Thank you, but surely I would be intruding?' floundered Frances, the invitation coming out of the blue.

'I expect you have something else planned,' Lady Ravenscar said gently, and suddenly realising that this was a way for the elderly lady to say a thank you for the assistance she had received, Frances made up her mind quickly.

'No, I have nothing planned. Thank you, I should love to come.'

Lady Ravenscar beamed her approval. 'Splendid! I shall look forward to introducing you to my family ... at least, those of them who are in town at present.' She held out her hand almost regally. 'You're a sweet girl who showed compassion for an old lady in distress. That is a rare thing these days, people are too busy rushing around to notice or bother. I cannot tell you how pleased I am that you called today.'

'I am too,' responded Frances, colour high, touched by the sincerity in the other's face and voice. 'I did absolutely nothing, but if it pleases you to think that I did ...' She smiled. 'I look forward to Saturday. What time shall I come?'

'Eight o'clock. Goodbye, Frances. Ring the bell and Simkin will come and let you out. Forgive me if I do not get up. Until Saturday ...'

Frances walked away from the house in a bemused state. What an amazing woman, she thought, going over their conversation. Gracious, kind, but beneath the frailty and charm was an underlying strength of character. How she must have disciplined herself to accept her illness, Frances conceded, coming to the conclusion that there was more to Lady Ravenscar than at first met the eye.

Frances hardly knew how she felt about the ensuing dinner party. The prospect of meeting new people never bothered her, and she had learned long ago which knife and fork to use! No, on analysing the situation she realised that it was the feeling of being swept off her feet by the deceptively gentle Lady Ravenscar.

Oh, well, she thought finally, one dinner party and then I probably won't see her again.

Zoe's reaction to the whole affair was one of momentary stunned silence, and then she burst into laughter.

'My God, Frankie, trust you! Widow of a knighted judge, of all people, and yet you said she looked aristocratic! I wonder who else will be there? You'll have to keep the flag flying—what are you going to wear?'

'I haven't got as far as clothes yet, Zoe, I've hardly become used to the idea that I'm going!' protested Frances, allowing herself to be swept into the bedroom where the entire contents of her own wardrobe, and that of Zoe's in the adjoining room, were inspected critically, Zoe's hands flicking impatiently through the hangers.

'The blue,' she announced at last, and: 'Yes, madam,' acquiesced Frances docilely.

Thus it was that she stood before the mirror the next evening giving herself a final inspection. Now that the time had come to leave she had to admit to a faint tightening of stomach muscles, rather like pre-stage flutterings.

Staring at her reflection, she wrinkled up her nose, conceding that Zoe's choice was probably the best. The blue was a silk jersey, deceptively simple, depending on the superb cut of the garment for its effect. Narrow sleeves helped to emphasise the long, slim line, the predominant feature being soft drapery around the neck. Frances slipped on her gold wristlet watch and carefully inserted tiny gold earrings. She ran a comb once more through her hair, tweaked a curl into place, smoothed the silk jersey over her hips and thought she would do. Catching up Zoe's sumptuous black evening cloak, she went down to the lobby to await the arrival of the taxi.

There was a row of opulent-looking cars parked out-

side the Ravenscar establishment. A lamp overhanging
the doorway illuminated the approach and climbing the
stone steps Frances felt a flicker of anticipation as she
rang the bell for the second time that week. Would this
evening be something special, she wondered, something
to look back on and remember?

As before, Simkin opened the door and smiled a greeting, taking her cloak and ushering her into the long green
room. She was conscious of about a dozen people, the
conversation level diminishing slightly as she made her
way through to Lady Ravenscar, seated in the same
winged chair. Frances smiled and took the hand out-
stretched to her.

'Good evening, Lady Ravenscar.'

The elderly lady looked truly magnificent. Dressed in
a black beaded evening ensemble which twinkled and
shone when it caught the light, adorned by diamond earrings, necklace and rings on her fingers, white hair sleekly
coiffured, and a face lightly rouged and powdered, Lady
Ravenscar retained Frances' hand, drawing her round to
her side to face the room.

'Frances, how lovely to see you again. How are you,
my dear?'

'Very well, thank you. I hope I'm not late, but the
taxi ...'

'I'm sure you are not, and in any case, we are still
minus one. Now—I had better introduce you to everyone. You will not remember their names, but never
mind.' and she proceeded to go round the room, Frances
smiling as each person was named, having to suffer Lady
Ravenscar's glowing account of her kindness in assisting
her the day of her illness in Regent Street.

'I'm afraid I have embarrassed Frances, but she should
not make light of her help. Gareth will endorse that, I
am sure.' Lady Ravenscar turned her attention away from
the group as a whole to one in particular. 'I will leave you

in the very capable hands of my doctor, Frances. Gareth, come and take Frances under your wing, please.'

The man thus autocratically addressed inclined his head to his hostess and obediently walked towards Frances, amusement on his thin face.

'Williams, Gareth Williams,' he said kindly, his dark eyes showing an awareness of her predicament.

Frances smiled. 'Yes, of course.' He was a Welshman, in his early forties, with an intelligent face, a fascinating voice with the suggestion of his native lilt, and a shrewd, lively manner.

'May I pour you a drink, Miss Heron? There's a selection, as you see.'

'Thank you, a sherry, please,' replied Frances, moving with him to a drinks table.

'I shall confirm Margaret's statement most sincerely,' he continued, selecting a glass and pouring, 'and I congratulate you on your quickness.'

'My father was a doctor,' she explained, 'and some of his knowledge rubbed off. I'm extremely glad that I was of use, but I do wish Lady Ravenscar wouldn't go on so about it!' she added in a whisper. Gareth Williams smiled knowingly.

'Margaret Ravenscar is a law unto herself, and a defiant patient, but I believe the message has finally reached her that her destiny lies to a great extent in her own hands and that I can't perform miracles above and beyond medical science.' He handed her the glass, raising his own. 'Your good health, Miss Heron.'

Frances responded, feeling warmed by the friendliness showing in her companion's face. She was retold the names of their fellow guests, the doctor adding a postscript when he felt one necessary. They were mostly relatives, with one or two old friends, and Frances realised that she was the youngest in the room.

They had barely worked their way round the guest

list when Lady Ravenscar rose to her feet, saying: 'I think we should go in. There's no telling when that son of mine will turn up and we will not spoil the food by waiting for him. Something must have happened to delay the boy. Lead the way, Bertram, and we will all follow.'

Bertram, described as brother-in-law and military gentleman, did so, looking slightly ruffled, and catching her eye, Lady Ravenscar gave Frances a rueful smile. As Frances approached she whispered: 'A career in the army leaves one with a liking for punctuality, I am afraid. Poor Bertram cannot say anything, however, for he knows that it would spoil my birthday.'

Frances paused in dismay. 'Oh, Lady Ravenscar, I didn't know!'

'How could you, child? Had I told you the reason for this little celebration you would have felt compelled to bring me something, and all I wanted was your presence.' Lady Ravenscar leaned gently on the arm Frances offered and they began to follow the remaining guests. When they reached the hall her hostess realised that she had left behind her evening bag and Frances returned to look for it. She found the bag pushed down the side of the winged chair and as she made her way back to the hall was aware that another guest had arrived. She hesitated in the doorway, not wishing to interrupt, noticing the pleasure on Lady Ravenscar's face and the warmth in her voice.

'Dear boy, there you are! I knew you would come, although you really are rather naughty, leaving it so late. Bertram has been simmering for the past quarter of an hour. We were about to dine without you.'

The 'dear boy' shrugged off his outer garment, handing it to a silently waiting Simkin. He then took Lady Ravenscar into his arms and kissed her gently, with great affection, on both cheeks.

'Sorry, Mother, something important cropped up that

I couldn't ignore. I tried to get out of it, but it was hopeless.' He stood back in admiration. 'You're looking marvellous! Younger than ever! Happy birthday, darling.'

'Thank you, son. As you see, I am wearing your ring,' replied Lady Ravenscar fondly, displaying a hand. 'It is a beautiful present.' Her eyes caught sight of Frances hovering uncertainly in the background and looking beyond him she added delightfully: 'Ah, Frances, my dear, you have found my bag, thank you. And now I can introduce Felix, my son. Felix, this is Frances Heron.'

The introduction was made with much aplomb, as if to say—now then, what do you think of that!—and the effect must have pleased her, for she gazed from one to the other with satisfaction.

Frances had the advantage, for she had recognized him immediately, standing rooted to the spot in amazement. *He* was the son! The man Felix was Lady Ravenscar's son! He was dressed very differently from the first time she had seen him—the immaculate evening suit and whiter-than-white shirt were a complete contrast to the black sweater and cords. But the set of the head and the easy, authoritative voice had not changed, neither had the topaz eyes. This Ravenscar son, as he slowly turned during his mother's introduction, veiled his reactions well, but not before she had seen his face show incredulity quickly darkening into brief anger.

Her smile of greeting wavered as she met the polite mask, and exchanged the murmured conventional words as his hand fleetingly touched hers.

Lady Ravenscar was saying: 'Here is Bertram come to see what is delaying us. As you see, the prodigal is returned, Bertram, and thank you, I shall take your arm with pleasure. Felix can look after Frances,' and giving them a smile she allowed herself to be escorted into the dining room.

Thank you very much, thought Frances in dismay, but

perhaps Frances doesn't want Felix to look after her, and judging from his face her feelings were reciprocated. As she began to move Felix Ravenscar detained her with a hard grip on her arm.

'Wait just one moment! I want to have a word with you,' he said grimly, swinging her back out of sight. 'What the *devil* are you doing *here?*' he demanded, his voice low and intense.

Frances stared at him helplessly, a confused set of emotions fighting for dominance within her. Everything was happening too quickly for her to grasp, but one thing was certain—this man was angry, and for some inexplicable reason, the anger was directed at herself.

'What is it? I don't understand . . .' she began.

'Who invited you here?' and he gave a furious shake.

A footfall made them break apart and Simkin's flat tones broke in to the sudden silence.

'We are about to serve, Mr Felix.'

'Thank you, Simkin, we'll be through in a moment.'

Face expressionless, Simkin inclined his head and walked into the dining room, tray in hands, and as he disappeared from view Frances said coldly :

'My invitation came from your mother, who did you think it came from?' and without waiting for a reply she made to go, shaken by the amount of suppressed violence emanating from him.

Laughter broke from the dining room and with a muttered oath, Felix Ravenscar said sharply :

'I'll talk to you later—it's impossible now.'

Frances stared. 'Always supposing that I want to talk to you, Mr Ravenscar!' She looked pointedly down at his hand on her arm and after a momentary hesitation she was released. 'If it wasn't for the fact that it would cause your mother distress, I would leave now. As it is, I will try and excuse your boorish manner and trust that you keep your hands and your extraordinary behaviour to yourself,' and on this note she left him and entered the dining room.

CHAPTER THREE

THE first course was being removed when Lady Ravenscar brought the conversation round to where she wanted it. In a lull in the proceedings she gazed down the table at her son, remarking with deceptive innocence :

'I expect you were surprised to find Frances here this evening, Felix.'

He looked up, glancing briefly at Frances sitting by his side, before returning his regard to his mother. 'Yes, you could say I was surprised, Mother.'

To put it mildly, thought Frances, and if she hadn't been so upset and infuriated, she would have laughed.

The remaining guests were looking interested and Gareth Williams, his methodical doctor's mind coming to their aid, spoke for them all.

'Do explain, Margaret. We were all surprised, and delighted, to meet Frances. Why should Felix be especially surprised?'

'And why should Miss Heron be thanked?'

This question afforded Lady Ravenscar immense pleasure, despite the formal use of the name. 'Because Frances is the young girl who helped me when I was ill,' she replied calmly.

Felix Ravenscar's composure was carefully maintained, only a slight movement of his jaw muscle denoted a momentary reaction. Frances' opinion of his acting ability, already high, went up another notch. She rejoiced inwardly. Now he could eat humble pie and like it!

'You *have* been enjoying yourself, Mother, with your little secrets, haven't you?' he said teasingly, and turning to Frances continued: 'May I add my thanks for coming so ably to her assistance that day?'

The sincerity of his voice jolted her, stabbing at the feeling of superiority and triumph she felt justified in showing as she returned his look, and she dropped her eyes to her plate, murmuring something non-committal. Then reason came to her rescue. Like any normal son, Felix Ravenscar cared for his mother, and would be quite naturally sincere in his thanks ... and that made no difference to her outraged feelings over the way he had acted on seeing her here. Why had he been so angry? She puzzled over this while tackling a delicious Dover sole.

Someone else was also doing some puzzling.

'You've lost me, Margaret,' complained Lady Ravenscar's brother-in-law. 'Where does the coincidence come in? Blest if I can see one!'

Lady Ravenscar's eyes twinkled. 'Frances belongs to the acting profession, Bertram.' She paused for effect. 'But the coincidence is more than that. She has just been given a leading role in a play to be serialised on the television ...'

It seemed that something was expected of her, so Frances gave a hesitant smile, aware of many eyes upon her, especially an unamiable pair on her right.

'... and Felix is to direct it,' Lady Ravenscar added gently.

Frances choked and gratefully took the glass of wine handed to her by the son of the house ... and by the time she had regained her breath the feeling of superiority had fled. As the amazing words sank in she turned and looked at him, unable to hide her dismay. As he raised his brows in question she whispered:

'*You?* You're the director of *Penruth*?'

'Yes. Didn't you know?'

'How could I know?' she demanded vehemently under her breath. 'No one told me ...' and her voice trailed and she turned her attention back to the sole, which now tasted like sawdust. Anxiety swept over her in waves, her mind flashing back to the audition to see if there had been any indication, however small, that could have given her a clue. It was hardly any consolation that she could find none. What right has the director to pass himself off as an actor! she thought in disgust, squashing the knowledge that she had assumed this and that he hadn't actually said anything to that effect.

What a mess! This arrogant, dictatorial, infuriating man was her boss!

Frances became aware that Felix Ravenscar was answering some questions about the play and then his mother said:

'I couldn't resist it, Felix. The anticipation of you meeting each other has quite made my day, and you nearly spoilt it all by being late!' She passed on her gaze to Frances. 'Do forgive me, child, but when you told me about *Penruth* I knew that Felix would be directing it and decided, quite on the spur of the moment, to give you both a surprise.'

'You've done that, Mother,' Felix Ravenscar said, giving his sardonic smile, and the meal progressed to general conversation. He turned a few seconds later, murmuring: 'It will look decidedly odd if you refuse to talk to me all evening. Try and make an effort, there's a good girl.'

Frances counted to ten. He's your boss, remember that, she told herself grimly. Your boss for the next ten weeks or more!

She said with tolerable composure: 'I'm quite out of polite conversation, I'm afraid.'

'Then try some that's impolite. I'm sure you'll have no difficulty.'

Frances took a deep breath. He didn't like her any more than she did him. 'Why were you so angry this evening?' she asked at last, deciding that attack was better than defence.

He hesitated and then gave a shrug. 'I thought you were using my mother as a means of meeting me.'

This was the last explanation she was expecting. 'I didn't connect you with Lady Ravenscar,' she said flatly. 'How could I when I didn't even know your surname? And if I had known it, there would have been no difference ... it would have meant nothing to me, nothing at all.'

'How devastating to my ego,' he replied whimsically. 'Do allow me to give you some more of this wine. I can recommend it.'

'I thought you were an actor,' Frances persisted, setting her jaw stubbornly.

'I was once. I cut my teeth in the live theatre, first as an actor, then as a producer.' He handed her the glass and she found herself sipping the wine obediently. 'I had the chance to work in television on a one-off thing, which was fairly successful. At that time the medium was young and expanding rapidly, new ideas were needed; I was asked to stay on and did so. Now that the industry is gaining maturity and the people in the top jobs firmly established, the openings are fewer. I was lucky to come in when I did.'

When he dropped his cynical manner the man was interesting, Frances thought, and very clever at changing the subject!

'You can't seriously ask me to believe that after being clasped to your manly bosom for a few minutes in a lift I formed an instant passion for you and devised the ingenious plan of getting myself invited here tonight?' She raised her brows incredulously and used her best drawl. 'Come, come, Mr Ravenscar—I can believe that you're aware of your masculine charms, but that's laying it on a trifle thick, isn't it?'

A vegetable dish was on its way round the table and appeared between them. When they had been served and the dish sent on its way, he replied:

'You'd be surprised at the things some actresses get up to,' and showing slight amusement in his voice, added: 'I didn't for one moment think that I personally was the attraction, purely my influence.'

'Really? Well, I can assure you that's not my line at all,' she responded cuttingly. 'Why didn't you say who you were when I told you I was looking for Tom Deverell?'

'I wasn't running the show. Tom was.'

She gave him a pitying smile. 'Oh, come, I'm not that naïve. I'm sure Mr Deverell discussed the auditions with you.' She paused and looked at him curiously. 'In fact, I don't see how I got the job. I received the distinct feeling that you didn't like me overmuch, Mr Ravenscar.'

'I never allow personal feelings to overrule business, Miss Heron. The casting of Mary Trewith was whittled down to between two, and you won ... Tom was struck all of a heap by the colour of your hair.'

She smiled sweetly, 'Which does *not* come out of a bottle,' and before he could speak further Frances turned her shoulder and became absorbed in the conversation on her left, Doctor Williams being only too pleased to include her in his discussion on the merits of a recent best-selling novel.

Frances finished the remainder of the meal not fully concentrating on what was going on around her, although participating quite adequately, or so she hoped. It was indicative of the man's personality that even against her will she was acutely aware of Felix Ravenscar next to her, and she was also aware of Lady Ravenscar's indulgent smiles as she periodically gazed down the table in their direction.

Obviously this son is the apple of her eye, thought Frances with grim amusement, and she expects me to feel the same way! She's in for a disappointment—and if the fleeting thought passed through her head that had Frances met him under different circumstances her feelings would be different, she crushed it. After all, there were plenty of men who had a good voice and knew how to use it, had charm—not that she had seen much of that!—were knowledgeable, amusing and showed a sharpness of intellect that was abrasive and stimulating. Plenty of men ... or so she told herself.

When she found herself next to Gareth on removing from the dining room, he brought the subject round to her new job.

'You're lucky to be working for Felix,' he told her quietly. 'He's an excellent director.'

'That's reassuring to know,' admitted Frances, touched by the other's kindly concern. 'I only know the reputation of theatrical producers.'

'From what I can gather,' Gareth went on, 'he's one of the top men in TV and the technical staff are all eager to work with him, which means something, you know ... technicians are good judges and only want to work with the best.' He smiled and leaned forward confidentially. 'Don't be put off by Margaret's obvious indulgence. Felix is a good son and worthy of her pride. I've known him, and his sister Jessica, for many years.'

Frances smiled back. 'You make a good advocate,' she teased, and later studied the two men as they stood side by side at the bookcase, in conversation. Although both were dark there the similarity ended. Felix was the taller of the two, and there was a lazy disregard towards undue movement as he rested his arm along the shelf, sipping his drink. Gareth had an unleashed energy just bristling to spring forth, never in repose for long, his hands moved expressively as he spoke, and his dark eyes were rarely still.

After a while Lady Ravenscar made a request for her son to play for them. Felix tossed back his drink in one movement and crossed over to her.

'I think the birthday girl should perform,' he told her, holding out his hand, 'after all, she's the most accomplished pianist among us.'

'No, Felix, not tonight. I am holding court and need to be entertained.'

'As court physician, Gareth, should I humour Her Majesty?'

Gareth gave him a push towards the piano, saying: 'Most definitely,' and he joined Frances on the settee.

'Do you play, Doctor Williams?' asked Frances, and he shook his head.

'No. I have no aptitude and no time.' He nodded in the direction of Felix who was settling himself at the piano. 'He could have been good had he concentrated on music as a career, but then Felix seems as if he could be good at anything he tackles!' and then they were silent as the piano playing began.

Frances lay back against the cushions, allowing the Chopin Nocturne to wash over her, half-closed eyes fixed on the figure at the piano.

As the last notes died away a spontaneous murmur of approval went round the room, but before it had a chance to grow Felix was encouraging Gareth to raise his Welsh voice, and needing no persuasion, Gareth joined him at the piano and they raced into some well-known and loved songs, with everyone joining in. Frances was quietly enchanted by the whole thing.

When the evening began to draw to a close, amid general goodbyes, she made her own to her hostess who gave her to understand that she was expected to visit again at the earliest opportunity.

'I realise that it will not be for some time, but I want to hear all about *Penruth* and Cornwall,' Lady Ravenscar announced, 'and your opinion of Felix as a director.'

'She's hardly likely to tell you that, Mother,' came the dry observation as Felix came up from behind with Frances' cloak, his own coat already on. 'And you wouldn't believe her if it wasn't complimentary,' he added teasingly.

'Oh, wouldn't I?' argued Lady Ravenscar, giving him a shrewd look. 'I know your faults only too well! Goodnight, my son, and God bless.'

'Goodnight, Mother, take care,' Felix said gently, giving her a kiss.

'You are driving Frances home, I hope?' his mother asked quickly, and he replied: 'Of course,' holding out the cloak and lifting Frances' hair free from the collar as she secured the clasp.

'Such pretty hair, Felix, don't you agree?' said Lady Ravenscar admiringly, and with complete composure her son replied:

'It is indeed, and not, I can assure you, out of a bottle.'

His mother looked horrified. 'I should think not! Why do you say that, Felix?'

He smiled and would not answer, merely drawing Frances towards the door, ordering over his shoulder: 'Now, Mother, don't come out, it's far too cold.'

Frances received a brief impression of Lady Ravenscar standing with a bejewelled hand to her throat, the other leaning slightly on her cane, a deeply satisfied look on her face, before she was herself hustled out.

Frances had made no demur regarding the lift home, knowing it was useless to argue. If Felix Ravenscar said that they would talk later, then talk later was what they would do.

She shivered slightly beneath the cloak as she waited for him to unlock the car door. It was a sleek black

Lancia, somehow eminently suitable to the image she was being given of this man—comfortable, high-powered but not overtly showy.

She turned and looked back at the house, dark now, and remembered her feelings as she had climbed the steps those few hours ago, wondering as she rang the bell what the evening held for her.

Now she knew. It held the knowledge that her future was tied up with a man who seemed determined to antagonise her.

'Miss Heron?'

Frances turned round to find that he was waiting, passenger door held wide, and as she climbed in she said: 'There's no need for this, you know, I could easily have gone home by taxi.'

When he joined her the remark was ignored and he asked calmly:

'Where do you live?'

'Lambeth.' Frances settled back, resigned, and had to admit that it was very comfortable and pleasant being driven home like this. She also realised, rather ruefully, that any righteous indignation she might have felt earlier by his unjustified anger at their meeting had fast dissipated beneath the soothing balm of good food and wine. Apart from the sticky beginning she had to concede that the evening had been very pleasant, and under such circumstances anger was hard to sustain. Especially as good sense ordained that if Felix Ravenscar was to be her boss then it would be madness to start off on the wrong foot. Here she gave a small sigh. She had already done that. Very well, it would be madness not to try and smooth things over between them.

His laconic: 'North or south?' broke into her reverie and she roused herself to say quickly: 'South ... near the County Court.'

'I know it.' He manipulated the car with ease through

the streets and there was silence until he swung into
Chelsea Bridge Road.

'I now realise that you were late for the audition because you helped my mother,' he stated at last. 'I am
right, aren't I?'

'Well, yes . . .'

'Which makes me very thankful that we didn't turn
you away unheard. That would have been on my conscience. I doubt we should be celebrating her birthday today had you not whisked her home as you did.' He
paused. 'You obviously must have realised that you were
putting the audition in jeopardy, yet you still accompanied her. There are not many who would be so un-
selfish.'

Frances supposed this to be a compliment, but it was
said in such a tone that indicated that the fact was hard
to credit. She looked out across the Thames at the lights
reflected on the water as they motored across Vauxhall
Bridge, and couldn't resist commenting: 'What a good
job you didn't know before, or I might have thought I'd
been given the part in *Penruth* as a reward for services
rendered!'

It was an unfortunate turn of phrase, bringing to mind
the fact that it was known for an actress to jump into a
director's bed and receive a part in consequence.

If her remark caused a similar picture he did not comment, merely contenting himself with: 'When you know
me better, Miss Heron, you will realise that no one, and
I mean no one, is cast in one of my productions other
than on merit.'

Which, thought Frances, was nice to know—if it was
to be believed.

Felix Ravenscar peered through the windscreen, saying: 'The Courts are ahead. Where now?'

She directed him and when the Lancia pulled up outside the house she said hesitantly:

'Thank you for the lift. I did thank your mother for the lovely evening, but if you could repeat to her ...'

'I apologise for my behaviour when we first met,' he interrupted rather brusquely. 'It was unpardonable of me. I jumped to the wrong conclusions and can only offer you the fact that I was irritable and out of temper through being delayed ... poor excuses, I'm afraid.'

Frances said nothing. For one thing she thought it only right to have her pound of flesh, and for another, he puzzled her. For such a self-contained man his anger seemed so out of character.

He carried on, undaunted by her lack of response.

'I'm often asked by hopeful aspirants what it is that constitutes a good director. I usually tell them that he is the central figure, the pivot, and from him determines good or indifferent television. He needs sound judgment, an ability to work well with all kinds of people, he has to inspire confidence and enthusiasm, organise yet be capable of delegating. He must keep his finger on the pulse, be responsible for everyone, be able to accept and reject advice and keep calm under any circumstances.' He gave a laugh and turned in his seat towards her. 'Of course, that's the *ideal* director, and no one man can possibly live up to all those conditions all the time. Pressures are brought to bear from all quarters in a job such as mine. I'm totally committed, Miss Heron, and accept these pressures for the most part philosophically, when I don't I shall know it's time to quit. But I'm human enough to become annoyed when something crops up out of the blue an hour before I have to leave for a special birthday party. Before I arrived tonight I had to organise a meeting with union representatives regarding the location work in Cornwall. We're dealing with thousands of pounds, a fact which can't be dismissed lightly, and any hold-ups on schedule could set us back a few more thousands.' He looked at her intently. 'Had the tensions of that meeting not been so great then I'm sure I wouldn't have over-reacted as I did when we first met.'

He was very persuasive. 'I understand,' Frances murmured.

He lifted a brow. 'Don't let me off the hook too lightly! My initial response must have upset you and could have completely spoiled the evening. Happily you had Gareth as a most admiring neighbour whenever you wished to ignore my insufferable presence, and the food was good, wasn't it?'

She looked at him suspiciously, but he remained straight-faced. Her own mouth, however, quivered.

'I think you're outrageous, Mr Ravenscar, and you know darned well I'm going to forgive you.'

'I admit I hoped ... you appear a kind creature.'

'Have you ever come up against something you couldn't cope with?'

He pursed his lips, eyes gleaming. 'I'll tempt the gods and say I don't think I have.'

'Heaven help those around you when you do,' announced Frances fervently, unclipping the seat belt and preparing to leave.

'Don't go yet ... there's something else that must be said.'

She paused at his words, surprised by the sudden change from whimsy to seriousness. He didn't speak for a moment, merely sat frowning out of the window, and then:

'My mother has a strong interest in you, Miss Heron, brought on quite naturally from the fact that she considers you saved her life ...'

'That's ridiculous, I don't want ...'

'... and she wishes to reward you suitably. She has certain ambitions that have now taken on a sense of urgency. It's her aim to marry me off, and now that she realises she's on borrowed time she has decided that blue-eyed, redhaired grandchildren would suit her plans admirably.'

'I think you're talking nonsense,' protested Frances feebly, trying to laugh it off. 'Why, I only met her properly the other day! She knows nothing about me!'

'I suspect she found out more about you than you did about the Ravenscars. Don't let the idea of a little old lady in lavender fool you, Miss Heron. Despite her ill health my mother is as tough as old boots. Once she knew you were cast in my play she started her planning, and the possibility that you could be cast in another part, one nearer home, was conceived.'

'I still think . . .'

'I'm thirty-six, Miss Heron, and according to my mother should have married long ago. She has lived to see my sister Jessica married and is aiming to keep alive long enough to see me tied up, good and secure. Then, so she says, she will be content to go. That I personally doubt. She is now, quite rightly, indebted to you and being a generous woman will bestow upon you the greatest gift she has—her son. Little realising,' he added, sardonically, 'that I'm no gift to any woman.'

'I still think you're being ridiculous,' was all Frances could find to say.

'I hope I am,' came the less than urbane reply, 'but having been through this situation a number of times, I doubt it.'

'If you've come through once you'll come through again,' she announced tartly.

'I know that . . . I wanted to make sure that you do.'

She took a deep breath. 'I wouldn't have thought you so conceited, Mr Ravenscar.'

He grimaced a smile. 'My dear girl, neither I am, but my mama has enough conceit for us both.'

'I see. Well, thank you for putting the matter so plainly,' said Frances. 'I take it that you have no inten-

tion of partaking marital bliss with anyone at the
moment? I mean, your remarks show a tendency towards cynicism that's hard to miss.'

'You take it correctly, Miss Heron. I have the mis-
fortune, some would say otherwise, to have been born a
realist. What I've seen of marriage during my life has
given me no desire to taste its delights.'

'And yet there are good, lasting marriages.'

'There are exceptions to every rule, but they're few
and far between.' He felt in his inside pocket and came
out with a diary, quickly turning the pages. 'Would you
like to have a tour of the studios one day next week?
Rehearsals begin on the Wednesday, so I suggest the
Tuesday morning, ten-thirty?'

Frances stared. 'I thought the whole idea is to dispel
your mother's romantic illusions—aren't you going a
rather odd way about it?'

'Not at all. There's no need to dash her hopes too soon.
You will also have the opportunity of finding out what
you will be coming up against when we start shooting.'

There was silence while they measured each other. At
last Frances said sternly: 'You're quite unscrupulous!'
and then giving a short laugh, added: 'Very well, I accept, but only because I would like to see the studios very
much. Where my career is concerned I can be unscrupulous too.'

'I can't believe that, I'm afraid, or you would never
have put your audition in such jeopardy,' he said dryly,
flicking the diary shut and slipping it back into his jacket.
'Good. Tuesday morning it is. I could pick you up, if you
like, say ten o'clock?'

Frances turned a mocking face, eyes bright. 'If I like?
Really, Mr Ravenscar, show some imagination, please!
Have a lift in a superb car as opposed to travelling by bus
or tube! What more could a poor working girl ask for?
I should be delighted to accept your kind offer, and ten

o'clock will suit me fine,' and because she mistrusted the
swift stab of anticipation that came with his offer, some
devil prompted her to add: 'You say you're not on the
look-out for a wife—might I not be looking for a husband? Between us, your mother and I might prove too
much for you!' and she moved to open the door to make
a swift and triumphant exit, only to find that it wouldn't
budge. After fumbling for a few seconds she burst into
laughter.

'It's not fair,' she protested, eyes brimming with mirth
as she turned to him. 'That was a superb exit line but my
timing's all gone now!' She pushed at another handle
and heard a click. 'Ah, that's the one, but it's too late, my
line's spoilt.' She tilted her head and added soothingly:
'I was only joking, you know. You needn't worry. I'm
not at all partial to dark men, and as you don't like red-
heads we're safe.'

'That sort of remark,' Felix Ravenscar pointed out
dryly, 'could be taken as a challenge.'

'It wasn't intended as one, I can assure you.'

'And are you on the look-out for a husband, Miss
Heron?'

She eyed him warily. 'No more than any other spinster
of this parish. Not any husband, though. I'm rather
choosy. I believe marriage is for keeps, you see.'

'The devil you do,' he murmured, searching her face,
eyes hidden by hooded lids.

Frances frowned. 'You say that as if you don't believe
me.'

'It isn't me you have to convince, Miss Heron,' he replied suavely, and thrusting himself from the car he
walked quickly round and opened the passenger door.
Looking up at the dark frontage of the building, he said:
'You'll be all right now?'

'Yes, thank you. Goodnight, Mr Ravenscar. Thank you
again for bringing me home.'

'My pleasure. Goodnight, Miss Heron.'

The Lancia did not move away until she was inside, and as she climbed the stairs to the flat she knew she was going to have difficulty in sleeping—so many thoughts and conjectures were whirling around in her head. She crept about as quietly as she could, going through the nightly rituals, aware of the sleeping Zoe in the next room. No matter where she guided her thoughts they always ended up with the same person.

Whether she liked the man or not, she had to admit he was a force to be reckoned with . . . and not easy to read. And how easy will he be to work with? she wondered rather worriedly, switching off the bathroom light and padding across the living room towards her bedroom. She paused at the window, thinking that at least it was a relief to know he wasn't going to play the part of Nick Penruth! and then a movement out of the corner of her eye made her turn with a start.

'Zoe! You scared me—standing there like that!' she gasped.

Zoe lifted her shoulders in an apologetic shrug. 'Awfully sorry, old thing,' she drawled, face deadpan, 'but I was mesmerised by the sight of you communing with the stars and pulling faces. Are you tight?'

'Certainly not,' retorted Frances, sweeping past and breezing into her bedroom. 'I'm sorry if I woke you, Zoe, but I tried to be as quiet as I could,' and throwing back the covers, she climbed into bed.

'Woke me?' questioned Zoe, following her into the room. 'Don't be daft! I haven't been home long myself, but if you thought I'd go calmly to sleep and not wait to hear how you've got on, hobnobbing with the aristocracy, you're mistaken—and don't you dare go to sleep, Frankie, before you can tell all!' she warned, giving her friend a prod as she sat at the foot of the bed.

'I'm not asleep,' soothed Frances, 'I'm merely resting

my eyes. You'll never guess who was there, Zoe ...'

'Well, whoever it was, you must have had a good time, it's nearly three o'clock!'

Frances sat up. 'Good heavens! It never is!'

'How the time flies,' cooed Zoe.

Frances ignored that and clasping hands round knees, said dramatically: 'The most amazing coincidence has happened, Zoe. Felix Ravenscar was there.'

'Good for him. Who is Felix Ravenscar?'

Frances sighed heavily, but seeing the ominous expression on her friend's face, went on quickly: 'If you fit Felix on to Ravenscar you get none other than the man in the lift!'

Zoe stared. 'Good lord! The dark sardonic actor?'

'Yes ... he just happens to be Lady Ravenscar's son—and Zoe, he's not an actor.'

'He's not?'

'No. He's a director! *Penruth* happens to be his production!' and Frances collapsed back on to the bed.

'Blimey! Wow!' marvelled Zoe, curling up under the quilt. 'Tell all,' she demanded.

Frances told her most of what had happened that evening relating it concisely and matter-of-factly, ending on the offer of the tour of the studios. She left out the anger on first seeing her, and the aspirations, maritally, of Lady Ravenscar.

'Quite an evening you've had, haven't you?' Zoe observed thoughtfully. 'This Ravenscar sounds dynamite to me. I'll see if I can find something out about him ...'

'... from your influential source?' teased Frances, quelling a strange reluctance for her to do so.

'This Gareth Williams ... a Harley Street man, you say? Now he would be worth cultivating. Is he nice?'

'Very. He's going to ring and arrange a theatre outing some time,' Frances told her mildly.

'Good!' and on that note of satisfaction Zoe wafted off to her own bed.

Sunday mornings the girls liked to lie in, reading the newspapers leisurely while eating breakfast. This usually took place in Zoe's room because it faced east and caught the morning sun, and this Sunday was no exception. Somewhere between the book reviews and the sporting page the telephone rang. No move was made to answer it from either of them, until after four or five rings Frances said plaintively:

'Zoe, it'll be for you.'

'How can you tell? And you're the nearest,' came the unconcerned reply as Zoe buried herself into the print.

'Oh, very well,' muttered Frances, 'but if it is for you, expect no mercy,' and she strode into the living room and picked up the phone, crisply enunciating their number. There was silence for a second and then:

'Frances?'

'Yes . . .' She caught her breath, and although she knew, added: 'Who is that, please?'

'Felix Ravenscar. I hope I haven't disturbed you?'

'No, not at all . . . I was just reading the paper.'

'I wanted to put your mind at rest. I've found your watch in the car, a link has broken in the clasp. You haven't missed it and been upset?' His voice coming over the telephone seemed deeper, even more attractive.

'No, I didn't know that I'd lost it! I'm so glad you found it. Thank you for letting me know . . . I would have been upset.'

'I'll have it mended and bring it along with me on Tuesday.'

Frances said quickly: 'There's no need to go to that trouble, Felix, I can easily . . .'

'No trouble.'

'You're very kind.'

'Yes, I am sometimes.' His voice was smiling. 'Until

Tuesday. Goodbye, Frances.'

'Goodbye.' There was a click and after a few seconds Frances replaced the telephone thoughtfully. She padded back to the bedroom, settled herself and found her place in the newspaper, absently reaching for her cup of coffee.

'It was for you, then,' said Zoe, still reading.

'Yes. Felix Ravenscar,' Frances told her, as though she received telephone calls from eminent directors every day.

Zoe's eyes lifted. She took in her friend's expressionless face and merely contented herself with a non-committal: 'Oh.'

'He's found my watch in the Lancia, a link has broken,' offered Frances after a moment.

'Lucky you lost it there, it would have been a pity ...' Zoe broke off suddenly, staring down at the paper.

'What is it?' asked Frances, leaning over to see, and with an: 'Oh, well, you'll see it sooner or later, I suppose,' Zoe handed the page over. Frances looked at the photograph and murmured: 'Mark.'

'Yes ... Mark Lucas portrayed as Henry V in the highly recommended Edinburgh production,' Zoe said with disgust.

'I'm glad things are going well for him,' Frances began, cut off by Zoe's cynical laugh.

'He's the type to fall on his feet, and if he doesn't he has a wife to comfort him!'

'You're too hard on Mark, Zoe,' asserted Frances quietly, 'but that's mainly my fault for not being able to talk about him.' She looked thoughtfully at the man staring up at her from the page, face in repose, and found with relief that she could do so without any emotional involvement. 'He didn't want complicity with me any more than I did with him. He was unhappy with his marriage but he didn't moan about it. You know how easy it is to play love scenes on stage and for this to overflow into real life. With living in each other's pockets for so long during rehearsals, wondering if the play was going to be a success, willing it to be one, we all became close. It's like living on another planet and what's happening outside becomes totally unreal and unimportant.' She sighed and smoothed the paper. 'It wasn't for some time that I realised how he felt about me and I felt so mixed up. When I was with him I was blissfully happy, but on my own all the doubts crowded in. If I could have gone to bed with him it might have helped, but I couldn't even bring myself to do that, let alone break up a marriage, even though Mark assured me it was crumbling long before we met.'

'So you left Chichester, where you were in a successful position, and joined a grotty second rate rep company.'

'Yes.'

'And he shoots off to Edinburgh and the next thing we know is that wifey has joined him.'

'Yes. So we're all happy,' said Frances firmly, and handed back the paper.

The heavens decided to open just as Frances left the building the following Tuesday morning. The rain hit the pavement with such force that it bounced up again, splashing her legs, and she dodged the puddles as she ran towards the waiting Lancia.

Felix Ravenscar leaned across and pushed open the door and she scrambled in, laughing as she fought the elements, finally pulling the door shut behind her. The wind had whipped tendrils of hair and plastered them across her face, and she sat, flushed and wet and out of breath.

'Hullo,' she managed at last, running a hand through her hair and turning to smile at him.

There was an air of crisp, clean smartness about Felix Ravenscar this morning—the cream shirt and brown pin-stripe looking as though they had just come off the rack. His dark hair was brushed into place and the faint sandalwood aroma of after-shave brought back memories of being in his arms in the lift, her head buried in his sweater.

The topaz eyes smiled and he drawled:

'I don't want you to catch pneumonia until after we've finished *Penruth*,' and a newly ironed handkerchief was flipped out of his top pocket and handed to her.

'I'll see if I can oblige,' answered Frances. 'I saw the car pull up and thought I'd save you getting drenched as well,' she explained, mopping herself up. 'This won't be much use to you now,' she observed, eyeing the now sodden handkerchief ruefully. 'I'll launder it for you, Mr Ravenscar, and ...'

He plucked the linen out of her hand and threw it negligently into the dash compartment. 'I thought we'd dispensed with formality on the telephone. You called me Felix on Sunday.'

'Did I?' said Frances in surprise that was genuine. She shivered slightly. The rain was now beating heavily upon the car, the water running down the windows in a steady torrent. The Lancia seemed isolated and very intimate.

'Yes, Frances, you did. And knowing how everyone is on Christian name terms in the theatrical profession, we may as well start practising today. Here's your watch,' he added, bringing an envelope from his pocket. 'Shall I fasten it for you?'

She nodded and held out her hand and he slipped it on, fingers cool and firm as he secured the tiny gold watch into place.

'Thank you for having it mended for me. How much do I ...?'

'There's no charge. One of our technicians did it— merely a ten-second job. Nothing that your independent soul could possibly object to,' and he smiled, a slow lazy smile.

Before Frances could check herself she found that she was smiling in return, the tensions of this meeting dissolving and a spreading warmth enveloping her. All her preconceived notions of behaviour for the day melted into nothing.

In that moment, as they sat smiling at one another, Frances was beset by a number of contradictory emotions, of which the first was exasperation. It seemed that she was completely unable to carry out the simplest of plans—of coolness and reserve. This was followed by the utmost pleasure at being on the receiving end of that smile.

Warning bells were signalling somewhere far back in the recesses of her mind, telling her that working efficiently with Felix Ravenscar didn't mean being a fool as well. That this man was a past master at knocking down the strongest of resolutions—and where was her backbone, for heaven's sake?

'How do you know that I have an independent soul?' she asked.

'I guessed.' His brow gave a comical quirk. 'Have you read any good horoscopes lately?'

She laughed. 'No! I only consult them when I'm stuck in a lift,' and feeling ridiculously pleased that he had referred to their first meeting, added teasingly: 'Was I right? About Scorpio?'

'If November the second comes under that sign, then yes, you were right,' he replied, peering through the windscreen at the now abating cloudburst. 'I believe it's letting up. I'll put the heater on once we're moving and you'll be warmer. Ready?' he asked, his eyes upon her once more.

Frances nodded and in the next moment they were under way.

So he had noticed her shiver, she thought to herself. Not much missed those eyes, and the reflection unnerved her slightly. She moved casually in her seat so that her eyes could rest on him without him being aware of her regard.

Scorpio ...

The sign of the Zodiac governed by the planet Pluto.

Scorpio ...

The sign depicted by the scorpion, whose sting is sometimes fatal.

You'd better remember that, my girl, Frances told herself urgently, and dragging her gaze away, looked resolutely out of the window.

CHAPTER FOUR

As they swung into Kennington Road, Felix said casually:

'My mother sends her love.'

Frances looked at him sharply. 'You told her you'd be seeing me today?'

'Naturally. It's given her something to think about,' he replied dryly, braking suddenly to avoid a motor-cyclist coming up on the nearside. 'Silly young fool,' he said calmly, watching the bike race on ahead.

Frances studied him curiously. There was no exasperation or show of temper following what could have been a nasty accident. This confirmed her first opinion that Felix Ravenscar was basically a cool customer, not readily given to displaying emotion, able to cope efficiently with any situation.

'How did you get into the acting game?' he asked suddenly, cutting into her thoughts.

She wrinkled her nose, giving the question her full attention. 'I suppose I drifted into it. A girl I knew at school dragged me along to a local drama group and it was ironical that her interest waned while mine grew. Leaving school at eighteen it seemed automatic to go on to drama school.'

'Your parents raised no objections?'

'They died when I was fifteen, but I don't think they would have stopped me going.'

He was quiet for a moment. 'Have you any brothers or sisters?'

Frances shook her head. 'No. I was transferred from day school to boarding school and from there went on to drama school. Luckily there was enough money to see me through my training, and by that time I was fairly used to being self-sufficient, so the rounds of grotty digs and strange, lonely towns were not hard to adapt to. The parts were small, of course, but I gained good experience —and when you're young it's all an adventure and part of living life to the full, isn't it?' and her voice was full of amusement at herself at that time.

Felix said dryly : 'Thus speaks the ancient twenty-five-year-old! You make my further decade seem twice that long.' He shot her a quick glance. 'And how different is the Frances of then and the Frances of now?'

'Five years different,' she said a trifle grimly.

'Do I denote a touch of cynicism in the tone?'

'Not really. You can't go through life without being hurt, can you?'

'Or hurting others.'

Frances frowned. 'Only unconsciously, I hope. Anyway, you don't go into this profession without realising the difficulties, not if you have any sense. I had my share of luck . . . I stepped out of understudy shoes into lead part on dress rehearsal night at Bristol—that was my first real break. I received good notices and the parts and the digs have become progressively better ever since. Hence me sitting here beside the well-known television director Felix Ravenscar.'

'Of whom you'd never heard,' came back the sardonic retort.

She looked at him thoughtfully. 'You couldn't care less about that, could you?'

He smiled but did not dispute her claim, saying instead: 'I believe I must have read your Chichester reviews.'

'You could have,' Frances admitted. 'We made the national press.' Her voice softened. 'That was quite a play.'

'I'm surprised they didn't keep you.'

Frances did not reply. She was dismayed by the sudden urge to explain, justify, but pride has two edges, and whereas she wanted him to know that Chichester had been reluctant to let her go, conversely she didn't want to make known the reasons for her flight. Luckily they arrived at the studios and this topic of conversation was shelved.

Felix parked the car and on their way into the building advised her of the morning's plans. 'I'm going to take you to a studio and leave you for a while. I've already checked with the director concerned and he's given his consent.' His stride faltered and he looked down at her quizzically. 'Will you chance the lift, or are you going to make me walk the stairs?'

She laughed. 'I'll chance the lift.'

'Good girl.' The doors slid open and they walked in. The lift behaved itself beautifully and they left it on the third floor.

'Here we are,' Felix announced, pausing at a set of double doors. 'In you go.'

Frances found herself in the control room of a large studio, looking very much as she had imagined it to look from information gleaned from films and documentaries. The wall opposite her was made of glass, giving a complete view of the studio floor below, where the actors and cameramen were working. All the technicians were wearing headphones and Frances could see a microphone standing on the long table area, through which contact was presumably made. It all looked, she thought with a flicker of panic, terribly complicated. She must have appeared slightly worried because the man seated opposite the microphone gave her an encouraging smile and lifted his hand briefly to Felix, who acknowledged the greeting and led Frances to a chair by the glass wall.

'I won't forget you,' he promised quietly, and resting his hand gently upon her shoulder in a reassuring gesture he then left.

She looked around her, feeling rather self-conscious at first, but as no one took any notice of her she gradually became engrossed in what was going on.

Her interest was initially held by the wall filled completely with monitored television sets, each showing a different picture of what was happening down below. She became aware that although the director and his staff, seated at the long table, had their backs to the glass wall and studio, they were following the action through these screens.

Turning to the studio floor she could see that it was divided into three compartments, or sets, each depicting a different scene. One looked like a pub-bar, another the kitchen of a modern house and the third a court-room. She had a bird's eye view from her position and was so involved that she turned in surprise when Felix slipped into the seat next to hers and she saw from her watch that an hour had passed.

They continued to watch, without speaking, until he touched her arm, indicating that it was time to go. On their way out he placed his hand briefly on his colleague's shoulder, receiving a lift of the hand in return, accompanied by a swift curious look in Frances' direction.

When they were out in the corridor Felix smiled and said:

'You look as though you're bursting with questions,' and she laughed happily, her glowing face raised to his.

'Oh, I am! I can't tell you how interesting I found it ... thank you, Felix ...'

'I'm glad the morning has been so successful,' he cut in smoothly, taking her arm and guiding her through a maze of corridors. 'You can ask as many questions as you like, but in comfort, with a cup of coffee,' and Frances found herself in a well furnished office where, at the press of a button, two cups of coffee appeared instantly and the deferential tone of the girl who brought them bespoke a certain amount of awe in relation to her companion.

This brought her up short for a moment, stemming the flow of questions, but Felix's politely effortless manner cleverly unleashed them.

'Who was the director talking to through the mike?' she asked curiously.

'To a man who we call the floor manager,' Felix replied, leaning back in his chair and crossing his legs. 'There has to be a liaison between the control room and the studio floor, thus the floor manager is a very important man. All instructions come from the director through to him, and he in turn relays this either to the technical crew, lighting or cameramen, or to the actors.'

'And the people sitting at the desk with the director?'

'The woman on his immediate left is the production assistant and she works ahead of the director, calling camera shots before they're due and following the script. She also makes arrangements for filming, travelling and hotel bookings, and keeps records of all decisions made.'

'Rather like a stage manager,' offered Frances, and Felix nodded.

'On the director's right are the two men who check the next shot due to go up and the colour levels.' He smiled at the look on her face. 'It sounds complicated but isn't really.'

Frances said pensively: 'I can understand now why a television director needs to know the technical side of things, but I suppose during rehearsals you work more or less the same as a theatrical director?'

Felix pursed his lips, giving the matter some thought. 'To a great extent, except that camera angles are always in mind.' He leaned forward and took her cup, placing it with his own empty one on the table beside him. 'Now, for the actor, the difference in the medium is rather like a painting. For the theatre the canvas has to be large, with strong brush strokes, emotions being conveyed by the voice and body. For television, the canvas is smaller and the brush strokes are delicate and intimate, emotions being conveyed by the flicker of an eyelid or the trembling of a lip—both of which would be lost on a theatre audience.'

They were interrupted by the ringing of the telephone, and with a murmur of apology, Felix answered it.

While he spoke, Frances thought about her morning. It had been a revelation and not only from the technical side. Her companion had showed her kindness and patience and as he was obviously a very busy man, the time he had allowed her was doubly precious. A busy man and one of importance—this had come noticeably to the fore by the respect shown him by others.

When the telephone conversation finished Frances half expected Felix to show some signs that the visit was over, but he settled back in the chair and ended her uncertainty by raising a quizzical brow, saying: 'Well? Anything more?'

She lifted her hands expressively from her lap, dropping them down again as she pulled a wry face. 'Too much to waste your time with this morning, but I would like to know how you start off on a project ... I mean, when, for instance, *Penruth* arrives on your desk!'

He nodded thoughtfully. 'We begin with a budget plan and call a planning meeting at which all the senior technicians, the head cameramen especially, are present.'

'Why are they involved so early on?' she asked curiously.

'To tell us if what we want to do can be done!' he explained simply. 'The moveability of cameras, lights, sound booms, all have to be taken into consideration. Then we cast and rehearsals begin. Any film inserts are done fairly early on to allow time for processing and editing. Towards the end of rehearsal time the crews come in and watch a run-through, to get the idea of the thing as a whole. Sometimes problems that were not considered at that initial meeting turn up and have to be ironed out. Rehearsals then move to the studio, make-up people come in; costumes, whether modern or period, have been under way during this period, and the dress rehearsal is run through. Finally the play is performed for the actual take.'

Frances grimaced. 'We'll skip over that bit—the thought terrifies me!'

'By the time I've finished with you, you'll have forgotten that the cameras are even there!' He rose to his feet, brow creased and head slightly tilted as he studied her. 'You might have some discomfort from the heat from the studio lights, and if the weather in Cornwall turns rough you may get rather wet,' he conceded dismissively. 'You'll be perfectly all right,' and seeing her face as she rose, added, 'What are you smiling about, Frances?'

She turned a demure face. 'You! How can I fail to be

anything but "all right" if you say so!'

He lifted a brow. 'I only surround myself with people in whom I have the utmost confidence.'

'You see?' she appealed, still smiling. 'Why, now I could fly to the moon if you said it was possible!'

He returned her smile. 'I won't be asking you to do that.'

Frances made her way leisurely home, stopping off to sit for a while in Park Square. The rain that had deluged over them earlier had ceased, and the sun had been out long enough to dry the pavements and benches, although the grass was still lush with moisture.

She sat for a while thinking about Felix. The words—I only surround myself with people in whom I have the utmost confidence—kept coming back to her. She hoped she could live up to such high expectations. But how typical those words were of the man! He would not suffer fools gladly, or waste time with people he didn't respect, she decided with wry amusement, neither would he kow-tow to people or conventions. She wondered what sort of a director he would turn out to be, finding that she was looking forward to the start of the rehearsals the next day, and on this optimistic note she caught the tube for home.

The following morning Frances allowed herself plenty of time to find the rehearsal room. She changed tubes at Oxford Circus and left at St John's Wood, walking in the direction of Prince Albert Road. She was wondering just how long they were going to rehearse in London before going down to Cornwall and was vaguely aware of a vehicle of some brightness passing her, but when this screeched to a halt, backing up for fifteen yards to finish broadside, the vagueness took a more solid form.

'Frank, girl! Light of my life! I thought I recognised that mop of brilliance . . . let me feast my eyes upon you.'

This enthusiastic and uninhibited greeting came from a

gentleman most adequately dressed for the car he was driving. Snazzy check sporting cap, long striped scarf, sheepskin coat and leather gauntlets in no way disguised his identity from Frances.

'Well, well, if it isn't Sir Galahad himself,' she teased. 'And what, my dear Julian, is this monstrosity?'

Julian Raynor took off his tinted glasses, pulled away the scarf and displayed a pained expression on his good looking face.

'My God, Frank! Monstrosity? Have you no soul, woman?' he demanded, flinging open the door with a flourish and unwinding himself with great dignity. Walking round the vehicle, his eyes feasting on its lines, he continued in a voice of utmost patience: 'This, my dear Frank, is the Panther Lima ... a stylish hand-built sports car, capable of travelling over a hundred miles an hour ...'

'Not with me in it,' retorted Frances, trying to look suitably impressed. Enthusiasm overtaking patience, Julian's words gained momentum.

'... four-cylinder engine, two twin-choke Dell 'Orto carburetters, a Firenza exhaust manifold ...'

'Yes, yes, Julian, she's beautiful and very striking,' Frances broke in, laughing, and he grinned, patting the long, low bonnet fondly. Knowing that Julian was a perfectly normal man, capable of intelligent conversation away from his cars, she took pity on him and stalked round the Panther, trying to look knowledgeable.

She had to admit that the whole effect was most impressive. The Panther Lima was blessed with a large, curvaceous bonnet and wings that flowed in graceful lines to old-fashioned running-boards. The two head-lamps, the radiator grid and the gleaming chrome of the bumper gave the appearance of a permanently grinning face, and looking at the bright yellow and black coach-work, Frances said dryly:

'You're easily identifiable, Julian! She looks like a wasp.'

'She certainly has a sting in her tail,' announced Julian, leaping back into the driving seat. 'In you get, Frank, I'll give you a lift.'

'Why, thank you, Julian, but it's hardly worth it. I'm nearly there, when I can find the place!'

'Jump in, I say. I know exactly where you're going,' and he gazed benignly up at her.

Frances stared back, hardly daring to believe him. 'Julian! Do you mean ...?'

He grinned. 'I do. It's time we worked together again, isn't it?'

Frances tumbled into the car and threw her arms round him. 'Oh, Julian, I *am* glad! Now I'll know someone in the cast. Who ...?'

'Nick Penruth himself sits before you, dear girl,' cut in Julian. 'All ready to tackle the first seven episodes and by popular request, a further twenty-seven!'

'Idiot!' exclaimed Frances, and suddenly realising the effect they were having on the inhabitants of Prince Albert Road, she said hastily: 'Does this thing have a seat belt, Julian?'

'It's damned difficult to get at,' he grumbled, complying with her request by finding it for her, 'and you're a gonner anyway if you have a bust-up.'

'You say the most reassuring things,' drawled Frances, clicking herself in, 'and Julian, I want to get to rehearsal in one piece with no speed records broken, understand?'

'The hall is just up the road, and if you think you can judge this beauty's potential by driving a hundred yards you're mistaken.'

With a 'whoomph' in the small of her back and a screeching bellow from the exhaust, the Panther sprang forward with a snarl, and Frances grabbed the sides of her seat.

They circled the area and finally whined into a car-park, windswept and exhilarated, with Julian shouting: 'It's got very good braking power.'

'I'm very glad to hear it,' Frances shouted back, and received his grin. Making a large sweep, Julian pulled up beside the line of cars. When the noise of the Panther died down they both eyed the sleek black Lancia, and raising his brows, Julian drawled:

'Very nice,' and jumping out he whipped off his cap, ruffling his fair hair as he walked round the Lancia for a closer inspection. 'I wonder whose this is?' he asked at last.

'Felix Ravenscar's,' replied Frances calmly, removing herself with some difficulty.

Julian stopped his prowling and looked at her with interest. 'Oh, yes? And since when has our Frank been carousing with the likes of our illustrious director?'

'Why should you assume I've been carousing?'

'Because you're beautiful, Frank, and Ravenscar has an eye for beauty.'

She dropped him a curtsey. 'Thank you kindly! What a lovely word carouse is. I wonder why we don't use it more often?'

'I make sure I use it at least three times a day,' Julian said solemnly.

Frances laughed. 'Fool!' He put his arm round her shoulders and they walked across the car-park towards the hall. 'Do you know him?' she asked casually.

'Who? Felix? Yes, he's a friend of the family.' Julian peered at her. 'How well do you know him, Frank?'

For some obscure reason Frances found herself colouring.

'Do stop looking at me like a dutch uncle, Julian. I don't know him at all—our relationship is strictly a business one.'

'Mind you keep it that way. Black Felix would make

mincemeat out of an innocent like you.'

'It's two years since Bristol,' Frances reminded him dryly, yet touched by his concern, 'and I'm a big girl now.'

'I'm very glad to hear it,' Julian replied disbelievingly.

As the first week of rehearsals passed, Frances knew that all she had heard in praise of Felix Ravenscar as a director was based on fact. Apart from his intelligence and intuitive flair for knowing what he wanted, he also had the ability to approach each actor in such a way as to obtain from them their personal best.

The cast was a large one and it was impossible to get to know everyone well, but those Frances came into contact with the most she found to be pleasant and friendly, and although they all worked hard there were lighter moments.

One evening, sitting in Zoe's dressing room watching her friend take off her stage make-up, Frances began to bring her up to date, relating a few amusing incidents.

'Who's this Gemma you keep on talking about?' Zoe asked, creaming her face.

'Gemma Ghent? Don't you remember, she was in that Scottish series about a year ago. Dark girl, very pretty. She's worked with Felix before and seems to know him quite well.'

Zoe's creamed face stared at her through the mirror. 'Oh?'

Frances looked back uncertainly. 'What do you mean, "oh"?'

Zoe shrugged. 'I mean that I've been hearing one or two things about your Mr Ravenscar, Frances. He might be the blue-eyed boy around the studios, but his reputation isn't all for directing plays!'

Holding out a box of tissues, Frances said carelessly: 'What have you heard?'

'Nothing terrible,' admitted Zoe, using the tissues with practised speed, 'he's not the flamboyant type, but he's left a few damaged hearts in his wake from females who thought they were the one to change his mind about bachelorhood. They all appear to have a good word for him, though, which says something.'

'How've you found this out?' Frances asked curiously, and Zoe flapped her hand.

'Oh, from one of his ex's ... and she'd come running if he crooked his finger again, by the sound of her.' She aimed the used tissues at the waste-basket and missed. 'She summed him up as being a clever, ambitious man who knows exactly where he's going.'

Frances picked up the tissues and dropped them in the basket. 'That sounds like him. He's working us as hard as hell so that we'll be ready to go south on time. When he's not sending us through our paces he's having consultations with the costume and make-up people, technicians and script-writers—the man's a positive dynamo.' She perched on the edge of the dressing-table and swung a leg. 'If he's as single-minded in his leisure hours as he is in his business ones I can understand why his ex would come running.'

'How did it go today? Was it as bad as you thought, being in front of the cameras?' Zoe asked, and Frances shook her head.

'It was as Felix said, we were so well rehearsed that after a few nervous minutes I almost forgot about them. Julian was a help, bless him.'

Zoe groaned. 'Oh, lor', Frankie, don't become enamoured of Julian Raynor! He has more scalps attached to his belt than Geronimo!'

'I thought you liked Julian?'

'He's good fun and the ideal partner for a party ...'

'I think you're wrong, Zoe. Julian may give the impression that he's hail-fellow-well-met without a care in the world, but he's not like that really.' Frances grinned mischievously. 'And he's driving me down to Cornwall!'

'Now you're showing some sense,' retorted Zoe cynically, covering her section of the dressing-table with a cloth and switching off the overhead light. 'Is it tomorrow that you're going to see the new Lowry play?'

'Yes, Gareth is picking me up at seven,' Frances explained, and Zoe shook her head wonderingly.

'And this is the girl who only a few weeks ago was saying she was off men!' she tossed over her shoulder.

'I didn't say I was going to live like a nun!' objected Frances, pushing open the stage door and taking a welcome breath of fresh air. 'I just said that I was going to remain heartwhole,' she added, coming to an abrupt halt.

'What's the matter?' Zoe asked, bumping into her and following her gaze. So far as she could see there was nothing out of the ordinary about the audience still streaming from the theatre foyer.

'If you want to see what Felix Ravenscar is like, Zoe, he's over there,' said Frances calmly, 'talking to the girl in white who looks like a model. See?'

Zoe peered in the crowd and then nodded. 'Yes, I see, and she's not a model, she's the daughter of a banker.' Her eyes moved over. 'So that's Felix Ravenscar,' she commented, watching the couple climb into a taxi and drive off. 'Mmm, an interesting face. I can see the attraction.' The two girls began to make their way to a Greek restaurant where they were meeting some of the cast from Zoe's show.

Zoe shot her friend a keen look. 'Are you sure he hasn't made a pass at you, Frankie?'

'Quite sure—and I'd know, wouldn't I?' Frances replied dryly. 'You needn't worry, Zoe, I'm quite safe. There's something about me that bothers him.' She shrugged. 'Nothing to do with the job. I don't know what it is.'

'Go down on your knees and thank the good Lord! because that man's nothing but trouble for a softy like you,' answered Zoe firmly, and following her into the restaurant, Frances was inclined to agree with her.

The Lowry play lived up to its expectations and Frances spent an enjoyable evening with Gareth Williams, the Welshman proving an intelligent and amusing companion, and showing a lively knowledge of the theatre. They parted with the promise of repeating their evening together when Frances returned from Cornwall.

Cornwall! Suddenly there was only one more day in London and then they would be off. Accommodation addresses had been given out, times of trains and buses had been noted. The tiny village of Morwenstow, the cliffs along that part of the north Cornish coast as well as Bodmin Moor, were all to be the main locations for the filming of *Penruth*, well trodden and loved by Frances in her childhood. Most of the addresses for the company to stay at had been in or around Launceston, a good central spot for that part of Cornwall, but they were not for her. Frances had high hopes of finding somewhere off the beaten track to stay.

With her mind buzzing over with plans, she ran down the last flight of stairs at the studios, turning over the idea of buying or hiring a bicycle for getting herself to and from the location points. She reached the foyer just as Felix walked out of the lift and they walked towards the main doors together.

Felix looked in surprise at his watch, saying: 'Good heavens, Frances, what are you doing here at this time?' They both said goodnight to the girl on reception, thanked the doorman for opening the door, and stepped out of the building.

'Wardrobe wasn't happy with a couple of my costumes,' Frances explained as they slowed to a standstill on the pavement outside. 'I've been having a fitting and it took longer than expected.' She looked at him and said impulsively : 'You look tired, Felix.'

He smiled faintly and replied : 'Will you come and soothe my fevered brow, Frances? Or is your cool palm already spoken for?'

'I wouldn't be much use, I'm afraid. I'd be fainting at your feet with hunger! I haven't eaten since midday, and that was only a snack,' she pointed out apologetically.

'So much the better. I dislike eating alone. May I feed you, Frances?'

'Why, I ... thank you,' and almost before the final words had stuttered from her lips she found her arm taken and she was led towards a waiting taxi.

'The Lancia is being serviced,' Felix explained as he sank into the back seat with her. 'They're bringing it back later this evening.' He ran his fingers through his hair as if to clear his thoughts. 'Any preference in the eating line?'

Frances shook her head. 'No, but I hope we're not going anywhere special? I'm not dressed for dining out.'

Felix passed a sweeping gaze over her silk blouse and tailored trousers, cream and brown, and the beige chunky-knit jacket slung round her shoulders.

'You look charming to me, but as we're eating in private you needn't worry.' Frances gave him a startled look and he added dryly : 'That is, unless you're too scared to dine alone with me in my flat?'

She felt the colour rise in her cheeks as she was given another glance, this time a faintly mocking one.

'No, of course I'm not,' she managed calmly, and with commendable panache, added : 'Do I have to earn my food by cooking it?'

He laughed with a spontaneous burst of amusement and Frances found herself laughing with him. 'By no means, my dear girl,' Felix told her reassuringly. 'I have a very satisfactory arrangement with an excellent French restaurant just round the corner. They deliver superb food at the ring of the telephone.'

'How civilised,' she responded with approval. 'Not even any washing up!'

The taxi pulled up outside a tall apartment block, quite old and gritty-looking on the façade but which, Frances soon realised, in no way advertised the comfortable accommodation inside.

She wandered over to the huge window where there was an unexpected view of the Thames in the distance. As it was nearly dark, the lights of the city added to the picture.

'I suggest you go and freshen up while I phone for the food,' said Felix, crossing to the telephone. 'The bathroom's through that door—have a shower if you feel like one, there's plenty of towels, but be as quick as you can, there's a good girl, because I'm ravenous!'

She grinned and ran. A quarter of an hour later she emerged feeling as good as new. Felix passed her with a 'make yourself at home' and disappeared into the bathroom.

The curtains had now been drawn and the table laid. Frances wandered over to the floor-to-ceiling bookcase which was filled to overflowing. Her eyes quickly passed along the shelves ... Conrad, James, Hemingway, Kafka, Hardy, Le Carré—none really gave a clue, except that his taste was catholic. The row of books devoted to the cinema and theatre was more expected, but the scientific and mathematical ones were a surprise.

'You've managed to keep happy, I see.'

Frances looked up with a start to find Felix entering, his hair curling slightly from the shower, looking less tired in a clean open-necked shirt and light-coloured pants. He moved indolently across the room, a bottle of wine in his hand which he placed on the table.

'I'm a compulsive bookcase scrutineer,' Frances confessed, reluctantly replacing a book on Picasso. There
was a ring at the doorbell and Felix glanced at his watch,
giving a nod of approval.

'Good. The food has arrived.' He left her and she could
hear voices in the hall. A few seconds later he reappeared
carrying a cloth-covered tray. 'If madam would care to
join me?' and with a swirl of the hand he threw off the
cover.

The food, as promised, was delicious and they were so
hungry it was eaten in almost total silence. The tray
was then restacked with the used plates and with wine
glasses refilled, they left the table and moved to the
other end of the room.

Felix paused at the record cabinet, selected a record
and by the time he had settled his long body on the carpet, his back against the seat of the settee, the mellow
voice of Sinatra washed over them.

Frances, curled up on the settee, pushed a cushion
over and fitted it under his head.

'What a clever girl you are, Frances, full of home
comforts,' he drawled, moving more comfortably to accommodate it. 'All I need now is the cool hand to soothe
my fevered brow.'

Frances had no intention of playing with fire. She
felt relaxed and happy and in complete control, and she
wanted to stay that way.

'Your brow doesn't look at all fevered to me, and if
it is then you should have chosen Diana Ross or Barbra
Streisand to soothe it for you. For me, Sinatra's fine.'

He smiled and made no reply.

From where Frances was sitting it seemed natural to
let her eyes rest upon him. The dark head was very close
to her knee. If she reached out she could run her fingers
lightly through his hair, or rest her palm against the

sharp planes of his face. His eyes were closed and she could see how thickly the lashes lay across his cheeks. One arm, sleeve turned back, was resting across his stomach, the other lay on the carpet, fingers comfortably touching the stem of the wine glass. With one knee upraised and the other outstretched, he lay in an attitude of complete ease.

The scorpion motionless, poised before the kill.

'What are you thinking, Frances?'

He hadn't moved, hadn't looked in her direction, but Frances felt a wave of panic sweep over her, almost as if he had caught her with her fingers actually touching the curls growing bushier because of the recent shower.

'I was wondering where you've managed to acquire that marvellous tan. Not, I guess, from our uncertain English weather!' She was rather proud of her casual tone.

'Quite right. I caught this filming on Corfu. Do you know Greece?'

Frances gave a spurt of laughter. 'Only from brochures, and it looks heavenly.' She gave a sigh, heavier than she intended. 'I'm not a travelled person. The furthest south I've managed is Land's End, and north, Middlesbrough!' Her shoulders began to shake with amusement. 'The mind boggles!' And then she said dreamily : 'Oh, but I'd love to go to the Greek Islands— or Venice—how beautiful Venice must be ... but then I've always had a yearning to see the Grand Canyon,' and her voice trailed, as if she was considering the toss of a coin to determine which dream should take priority.

'I've seen most of the places I've wanted to see,' Felix said pensively. 'I'm afraid I tend to take travel for granted these days, business or pleasure. A pity when the bloom goes off enthusiasm.' He took a drink. 'You would be an excellent companion for the blasé traveller, Frances. Your delight would renew all the old ones. I should like to take you to the Greek Islands, or Venice, which though very beautiful is a dying city and rather sad. Would you come with me, Frances, and make me see them through your eyes?'

The words dropped like a stone into a pond, the ripples multiplied in ever-increasing circles. Shock ripples.

Frances sat very still.

'Of course, if you'd rather it was the Grand Canyon, then Arizona it shall be, but I'd sooner you chose Greece or Venice—both are much more romantic than the Grand Canyon.' He opened his eyes and twisted his head slightly. Sinatra was adding to the occasion by begging her to fly with him to the moon. Both requests were equally outside her scope.

'Have you lost your tongue, Frances?'

The tawny eyes held hers in a steady look, clear and questioning, and Frances dragged her own away, transferring them to the wine left in her glass.

'You shouldn't joke about such things, Felix,' she scolded gently, 'you might be misunderstood.'

'I'm not joking, my dear. I was never more serious in my life.'

'I ... I don't believe you.'

'I wish you would.' He turned his body towards her and took her free hand in his, caressing the smooth skin of her inner arm with his fingers. 'We'd go to Corfu first, I think, it's an ideal place to get to know each other. Life is leisurely on the Island. We would lie on the sands in the sun, swim in the bluest of blue seas, drink local wine beneath the moon ...'

'You *are* serious!' Frances whispered incredulously, pulling away her arm as if she had been stung.

'But of course, I've just told you so,' and now his eyes were watchful.

Her whole body was tingling with the shock and she
fought for self-control.

'I know actresses are supposed to be free with their
favours, but just what makes you think I'd go with you,
Felix?'

'I don't know for sure. That's why I'm asking you.'

'I see.' She took an impatient breath. 'I must be especially dense this evening ...' She stopped and then began
again. 'You must, then, consider I would be willing to
share your bed. I can't see you being content with only
listening to adjectives of praise on the surrounding
countryside.'

His lips gave a sudden quirk in appreciation of her
comment, and he rose and strolled over to the mantel
where he placed his glass.

'You're right, Frances, but I wouldn't rush you. I'd
let the sun and wine and the sea and the magic of the
island wash over you until you wanted me as much as I
wanted you.'

'You think that would happen?' she asked between
dry lips.

He gave a slight shrug. 'I'm quite sure it would.'

Anger was to be her only weapon. It cut through the
stupid ache in her throat.

'I suppose I should feel flattered ... you're very sure of
yourself. I think I ought to tell you, Felix, that though
as a television director I respect and admire you very
much, as a man I find your conceit very hard to swal-
low.' She finished off the remainder of the wine with a
flourish and placed the glass carefully on the side table.
She swung her feet to the ground, looking vaguely round
for her discarded shoes. 'And now I think I'd better
go.'

Standing up was a mistake. It brought her much too
close to him, and as she was shoeless he now towered
above her, making her feel small and vulnerable. She

had no fears for her bodily safety. Felix Ravenscar was far too smooth a customer to abuse a guest's hospitality. It wasn't him she was scared of, and he knew that.

'Man is a conceited animal, Frances, and where two people who are attracted to each other are concerned, the conceit is forgivable, surely? You don't dispute that there is an attraction?' he asked evenly.

She stared up at him, her colour deepening, eyes wary. 'I ... I don't know what you mean. I've never ...'

'There's an easy way to prove it,' and his hand lifted, fingers gently touching the outline of her cheek.

Frances caught her breath, feeling the flesh scorch, catch fire, and despite the defiance in her gaze as she met the lazy, tender amusement in the tawny eyes, found herself trembling, powerless to speak or move.

Without touching her he began to kiss her, tiny tantalising kisses at first, brushing lightly over her exposed skin, returning again and again to her lips, lingering longer and longer. Only when she swayed slightly did his arms go round her, holding her against him, and as the sweetness and the pain welled up inside her for one despairing moment her mouth moved beneath his, giving the response he was demanding.

Almost she could believe it real ...

He was drawing away and the sweet torture ceased. She could feel his breath on her cheek and heard his low: 'Have I opened your eyes to yourself, Frances?' and his lips touched her lids briefly. He held her away and as her eyes opened, slowly as if drugged, his own searched her face.

For a long moment their gaze held. Had he shown any sign of triumph she would have shrivelled up with mortification. But Felix was too much a man of the world, too well-mannered to say I told you so! Too knowledgeable about the way bodies were treacherous things and not to be trusted to show anything other than his usual enigmatic face which seemed, at this moment, to be carved out of granite.

His hands were steady as he poured out another drink, his voice controlled as he asked her if she would like another, an offer she refused with a bemused shake of the head.

Not for him had there been world-shattering revelations. Not for him had the earth rocked on its pivot. She wished she had the strength and the nerve to throw the wine in his face. She wished ... oh, God, she wished he had a heart!

She sank to the settee and found her shoes, slipping them on, knowing that he was watching her a few yards away. She rose and took a deep breath.

'Thank you for the eats and drinks, Felix.' Hell! she thought in disgust, you sound like a small girl leaving a kids' party! Remember to say thank you to the kind gentleman! she mimicked silently.

She gave him a quick look and saw a flicker of amusement in his eyes and she carried on quickly: 'As for your generous invitation to Corfu, I'm very flattered, really I am, but I'm sorry, I have to turn it down.'

The gleam disappeared and a watchfulness took its place as he said mildly: 'May I ask why?'

'Yes, of course, that's only fair.' She lifted her chin and made herself look at him fully, her eyes wide and steady. 'You were right about the attraction, you've just proved that, but it doesn't make any difference.' She even managed to allow amusement to creep into her voice. 'We'd be fine in bed, with the wine and moonlight as extras—I'm sure you're a very experienced lover, Felix, but I'd completely ruin the sun, sea and sand for you with my guilt complexes.' She paused and he took the cue beautifully with a bland:

'Guilt complexes?'

'Mm ... not the marriage lines! Nothing so old-fashioned as that! and I quite understand that you don't want to feel responsible for anyone but yourself, total commitment is not for you, is it, Felix? No, it wouldn't be the lack of a ring ...'

There was no indication that her words affected him in any way. His voice was smooth and quiet. 'What would it be, Frances?'

'The pretence,' she said simply. 'I have to believe in what I'm doing, you see. I'm sure I could be stupid enough to fall in love with you, if you gave me half the chance, but I would want you to love me in return ... mean it, say it, even knowing deep down that it wouldn't last.' She shrugged her shoulders slightly. 'And you're not prepared to say that, I know, and I quite understand.'

If she had surprised him he didn't show it. The telephone rang and while he answered it Frances found her jacket and handbag. He replaced the telephone, stood looking at her with penetrating steadiness for some seconds and then said:

'That was the garage, they've delivered the Lancia. I'll take you home.' He picked up his jacket and slipped it on, crossing the room to stop in front of her. 'If you ever succeed in killing off those guilt complexes, Frances, let me know and we'll be on that plane before you can catch your breath!' and lifting her chin with his hand he gave her a short, hard kiss, and then pushed her gently towards the door.

As it closed behind them, Sinatra could be heard singing—There's no such thing as make believe—his voice full of sadness and longing.

CHAPTER FIVE

FRANCES stopped for a moment to take a breather, brushing a strand of hair from her face, turning her eyes back to the way she had come. The climb had been stiffer than she had expected, but the view from the headland was worth it. It was nine-thirty in the morning, the whole day spread before her to do with it just what she liked. In her canvas bag she had fruit, swimming costume and towel. Padstow lay to the north and Newquay to the south, but neither of these was her aim.

She had hitched a ride on a lorry at seven that morning, picking it up on the Bideford road. She had an enjoyable chat with the driver who was pleased for company in any form, especially when it was a young and friendly girl who looked as though she had stepped out of the pages of a health and beauty magazine! For the eight weeks spent working in Cornwall had given Frances an added bloom. The sun had kissed her fair skin and turned it golden, and bicycling to and fro had made her very fit. But she had left her bicycle at the farm today, intending to walk the coastal path, but first she had had to reach the coast itself.

The lorry driver had wanted to turn off his route and take her right into Padstow, but she was able to convince him that it wasn't necessary. Waving him goodbye, she then set out along the lanes, the sea somewhere ahead of her, following her map. Leaving St Issey and Little Petherick behind, the lanes were even narrower than before. She was glad of a lift on the back of a farm tractor and left it two miles further on as it turned into field gates. Now she could see the sea in the distance and with renewed enthusiasm she lengthened her stride.

And here she was, an hour later, taking a breather and

feasting her eyes on the coastline. Memories were coming back to her, for this was another journey into the past, bringing with it a faint pang of loss.

She decided to sit down for a while and eat an apple— the bacon sandwiches that the farmer's wife had prepared seemed a long time ago. The sun shone on the sea and she narrowed her eyes, trying to imagine what lay beyond the horizon. Newfoundland? Labrador? Her geography wasn't good enough to make an accurate guess. What would it be like, she wondered, to take a boat and just sail out until land was sighted?

She took a firm bite of the apple and crunched hard, enjoying the crispness and juiciness. She wouldn't think of travel and distant lands. If she did, then the island of Corfu would creep into things, and if that did, then someone else would creep in as well.

It was quite permissible to think about the job. Frances tossed the core over the cliff edge and lay back, finding a patch of rough grass that wasn't smothered in prickly gorse. Yes, the job was fine, terrific, in fact. The weather had been kind and now here they were in June, and it promised to be hotter still. Three scenes were left to film ... in one week they should be finished, and back in London. And she would be sorry. She gave a sigh and sat up.

Heavens! Frances Heron, don't you know by now that all good things must come to an end? she asked herself crossly, rising to her feet and brushing herself down.

Striding off along the cliff path, Frances grimaced at the tiny scratches on her legs from the overhanging gorse ... the path was barely a path at all in some places along the route. She realised that she should have worn jeans to protect herself, but it had seemed the day for shorts, and it was—for those sensible people on well-kept pathways!

The going was fairly easy at the moment, however,

and as she walked she thought ahead to the next day's shooting. It was to be the boat scene and she wasn't looking forward to it one bit. So much so that she was wondering whether she should ask Felix to allow her stand-in to do it, but even as the idea came she rejected it. He would think she was being awkward, especially after yesterday's tussle over the cliff climb.

Even now she could hear his furious voice as she was met at the top of the cliff by a livid Felix, just because, contrary to his orders, she had taken the more difficult route up the face of the cliff. This route had been first picked out as being a good one and then Felix had decided it was too difficult and wasn't safe. Frances thought otherwise and merely changed course half-way up the climb when it was too late for anyone to do anything about it. That Felix had nearly been proven right hadn't helped. She hadn't taken her long skirts into consideration, but she had achieved the top and had waited triumphantly for praise that hadn't come. Instead, his words had lashed out at her for being foolhardy and pigheaded, and others stronger, which afterwards made her realise just how angry he had been. She was glad that the crew were not in hearing distance although it was apparent to all what was going on. The only good thing about it was that Rick, who was the head cameraman, was convinced that the scene would be terrific, far better than they had hoped.

Rick told her this later on in the pub where the company all used to meet. The bar had been crowded, the locals having a friendly darts match with the studio team, and as she walked in with Julian, Frances had seen Felix standing at one end of the bar. She wondered if he was still angry with her and thought he must be, for he looked up, caught her eye across the heads between them, but made no sign of acknowledgment She was glad that Julian spoke to her at that moment so that

Felix couldn't see her face, which she knew had gone red.

Rick waved a hand from his corner and she made her way over, arriving breathless and laughing because of the passing comments. She got on well with the crew, they all liked her professionalism, silently applauding her lack of artistic temperament and the way she tackled re-takes without a fuss, and the locals liked her genuine love of their countryside and historic past.

'Do you want a drink, Frances?' Rick asked when she sat down at the table, but she shook her head.

'Thanks, Rick, but Julian's getting me one,' and she turned to see Julian's fair head making for the bar.

'How are you feeling after your climb?' Rick asked, and then grinned.

Frances pulled a face and grinned back. She liked Rick. He was short and stocky, middle fifties, with iron grey hair sprouting from a balding head. A Scotsman, married with grown-up children, he and his wife had brought their caravan down to Cornwall, both taking an interest in Frances. She had spent many enjoyable evenings talking in their caravan.

'You could have hurt yourself,' Rick said in a fatherly manner. 'And when you stopped half-way I thought you were stuck there for good.'

'Oh, there was no real danger,' breezed Frances. 'I was merely taking a rest. I've climbed far worse cliffs in my time—no cause for panic.'

Rick whistled through his teeth and shook his head.

'You wouldna' have thought that if you'd heard the boss watching you! On second thoughts, it's perhaps as well you didna' hear him—he used some choice expressions, a few I'd not heard before! Thought you were going to be torn to pieces, lassie, when he saw you get safe to the top and strode after you. Maybe the fact that it took some time to get up to you saved you,' and his face creased with amusement at the memory.

'If it had been the last day of shooting he might have done,' Frances said gloomily, eyeing the silent man sitting by the bar with a dour look, 'but no doubt he remembered his precious schedule.'

'He said plenty, eh?'

She nodded. 'But then so did I.'

'Och, he's a good man, and you're a sore trial to him, lass.'

She straightened, indignant. 'Oh, Rick, how can you say that! Why, the cliff climb's the only thing that's upset him, surely?'

'He wasna' very keen on you riding the chestnut ...' Rick began, breaking off as Julian arrived, triumphantly placing the drinks on the table before them.

'This must have been a nice quiet pub till we came,' he announced cheerfully, pulling up a chair and pushing one of the beers over to Rick.

'Thanks, Julian,' Rick replied, taking a long thirsty gulp. 'And then there was the bull,' he added to Frances.

'That's not fair, it wasn't my fault. I didn't know the darned bull was in the field and I couldn't hear what you were all shouting,' she defended.

'What's this then? All your misdeeds, Frank?' teased Julian, his tanned face grinning widely.

'I don't know what you'd all talk about if I didn't provide you with something,' Frances said airily, 'and if you want to win at dominoes tonight, you'd better look to your laurels, for I'm feeling lucky!'

A few moments later she saw Gemma talking to Felix and the next time she looked they had both disappeared. She lost the game of dominoes, and the next two ... the luck was all against her.

Frances was brought back to her present surroundings by the sight of fellow humans coming towards her and they exchanged pleasantries and continued on their way.

The sun was getting higher in the sky now, and more people were abroad, although the cliff tops were still comparatively deserted. The coastline was full of sandy coves, small and isolated, cut off when the tide was high, but accessible at the moment either by a long trek over the rocks from the main beaches, or by a fairly arduous climb down the cliff face.

Crossing another headland Frances could now see Bedruthan Steps in the distance—that was her goal. She would sit for a while and watch the sea creaming round the huge rocks, and then continue a little further along the coast to one of the small coves, where she would settle herself for an hour or two before making her way back.

There was a smattering of cars in the car-park, but the visitors were spread out and she found a spot to herself on the springy grass where she sat down. Hardly there for more than a few moments she heard steps behind her, and feeling rather annoyed that out of all the stretch of cliff someone should invade her territory, she turned round with a frown on her face. The frown was met by another, one more pronounced, and her heart sank. Oh, dear! She was in trouble again, by the look of things. She smiled, replacing the frown and said in surprise:

'Why, hullo, Felix! What brings you here?'

'You do,' came the uncompromising answer as he stood a couple of yards away, looking down at her.

'I do?' She patted the turf invitingly. 'Won't you sit down? I shall get a crick in my neck if you don't.'

'You're lucky I don't wring it!' he said grimly, but sitting down nevertheless. He was wearing a white T-shirt which fitted snugly, accentuating the latent strength in his shoulders and the breadth of his chest. His arms and face were very brown. She couldn't see the expression in his eyes because they were hidden by sun-glasses, but she could give a fairly accurate guess.

She gave a small sigh and turned back to the sea, resting her chin on her knees, bare arms clasping bare legs.

'What have I done now, Felix?'

'You really are an infuriating woman, Frances! You seem to do things deliberately to annoy me, and it's got to stop.'

Frances swung round. 'I don't know what you're talking about! How have I annoyed you today, for goodness' sake?'

'You were supposed to have met Rick and myself this morning at eight-thirty, if you remember, to have a practice run with the boat! If you'd already had plans why the hell couldn't you have let me know!'

'Because I knew nothing about it, that's why! Honestly! Do you think I'd deliberately ...'

'I didn't think you'd mess Rick's day off, but I have no doubts you not minding about mine! Why didn't you say ...?'

'Because I wasn't told, that's why, and if you don't get that into your thick skull, I'll ... I'll ...'

'Just go ahead, Frances. I'm in the mood for physical violence! Sitting waiting for you to turn up here, wondering if, in fact, you would, hasn't improved my temper!'

With an exasperated exclamation Frances threw herself back on to the turf, staring fixedly up at the sky, arms behind her head. She gritted her teeth and concentrated on calming her turbulent feelings. At last she said quietly:

'Who did you ask to tell me, Felix?'

She saw him give a quick frown. 'Gemma.' He took off his glasses and swung them between his fingers as he stared down, eyes narrowed.

'Well, she didn't pass on the message,' Frances said flatly.

'Rick rang her this morning to check and she says she did.'

She held his gaze and said slowly and distinctly: 'At no time has Gemma given me that message.'

'Why would she lie?'

'I don't know ... perhaps she thought she'd told me,' and perhaps she knew she hadn't, Frances thought to herself. There was no love lost between Gemma Ghent and herself, but she had no intention of telling Felix that. She sat up and added indignantly: 'You don't think I'd purposely do it, do you? Do you, Felix?'

There was a pause, and then: 'Rick doesn't think so.'

'But you do!'

'Strong words were passed between us yesterday, Frances. It could have been a way of getting your own back.'

'How could you think that!' A lump stuck in her throat and she turned her face away, struggling for composure, tugging at a tuft of grass with trembling hands. Then she got to her feet, grabbed her bag and mumbled: 'We'd better get a move on, hadn't we?' and when Felix said evenly: 'It's too late now,' she stopped and face still averted, asked: 'Why?'

'Because the tide is all wrong now, that's why.' She heard him get to his feet and come over. 'We shall have to start out earlier tomorrow and have a go then.'

She nodded, not trusting herself to speak.

'There's another thing,' Felix continued. 'I didn't say anything when you plonked yourself down in the middle of nowhere, careering round the countryside on that bike. I considered when you turned up late for work would be time enough to haul you back to civilisation. Well, you haven't been late once and seem to have survived, but that hasn't made it any easier to put up with. You were an added worry being so far away from the rest of us.'

'I wasn't the only one off the beaten track,' she muttered.

'I know, but you were the only one on her own, without a car, without a phone.' He paused, took a breath and made his voice more reasonable. 'Anyway, don't you think it would have been sensible to have told someone where you were going today? What would have happened if something had gone wrong? If you'd fallen and hurt yourself, miles from anywhere?'

'It would hold up your precious shooting, wouldn't it?'

There was silence.

'And now it's you who is misjudging me,' he said slowly.

Frances swallowed hard. 'I'm sorry. I didn't mean it.'

'There's enough truth there to plead justification. With so short a time to go I always get a bit shirty about accidents, I must admit, but I'm more concerned about your personal welfare than the programme.'

Frances scuffed a toe against a clump of heather. 'I told Farmer Bill. He knew where I was going.'

'And he told me—when I at last ran him to earth, ditching on the furthest part of the fields.'

'Oh! I'm sorry,' she said faintly.

'So you should be. I had to walk across four fields to find him, wasting precious time. If I'd met you then I don't think I should have been answerable for my actions,' Felix said grimly.

Frances blinked hard as she tried to focus on the rocks jutting out to sea. 'I'm sorry you've had a wasted morning, but I really didn't know you wanted me, and if you won't believe me, you won't,' she answered in a tight little voice. Felix took her by the shoulders and turned her to him. She couldn't look him in the face and concentrated on the thick leather belt encircling his waist. One hand left her shoulder and a finger lifted her chin.

'Dear me ... I never thought I'd see Frances Heron shed tears, I thought she was indestructible. This will never do.' He fetched out a handkerchief and wiped her lashes carefully. 'Shall we call a truce?' he asked gently, and she nodded, a wave of thankfulness sweeping over her. Felix drew her to the grass and for a moment they sat together in silence, then he gestured to the rocks. 'Tell me about them. I'm sure you must know something.'

Frances was hugging her knees again, glad of something straightforward to talk about, her eyes searching the huge rise of gigantic rocks, green-capped on grey.

'They say the rocks were stepping stones for the Giant Bedruthan, but I don't know anything about him. That rock over there,' and she pointed a finger, 'is called Queen Bess, it's supposed to look like her from a certain angle, and the other one has a woman's features too, can you see?'

'An awesome place, even on a sunny day like today,' Felix mused. 'I wonder what it looks like in winter?'

'Wonderful,' returned Frances warmly, 'but it *is* treacherous. Quite a few people have lost their lives swimming from the rocks and it's banned now.' She plucked at the grass again, watching the slight breeze taking the strands from her loose fingers and tossing them over the cliff edge. 'What are you going to do now?'

'Share a most admirable picnic lunch with you,' he studied his watch, 'and by my reckoning it's lunchtime right now. He looked round the cliff-top. 'The beautiful weather is attracting the crowds. Shall we find somewhere quieter to eat?'

'I already have my lunch,' said Frances, a glow of surprise touching her cheeks as he pulled her to her feet. He handed her the shoulder bag, saying:

'By the feel of that, there's not enough for me to share,

and I've brought wine!' His smile flashed. 'Begin to walk slowly along the cliff and I'll catch you up.'

Frances watched him jog back to the car-park, her spirits lifting. Damn Gemma Ghent and her stupid jealousy! Didn't she realise that she had nothing to fear from Frances? There Gemma was, sharing the same hotel as Felix, sharing the same breakfasts and evening meals, more than likely the same bed, and she had to be-grudge Frances an unscheduled morning out in a beastly boat, chaperoned by Rick! The thought was laughable. There was no cause for jealousy, but Gemma was a care-ful soul and who knows, perhaps some sixth sense might have told her there was something there between them. Everyone else, however, thought Frances was Julian's girl, and in a way, she was. They both worked and played well together, had exchanged kisses in the sun on the beach and under the moon in a country lane. They had held hands in the cinema and raced their horses along the seawashed sand. Julian, for Frances, had been her saviour.

Not that Felix had been anything other than her boss since that memorable evening, had never sought out her company during leisure hours, had treated her with the utmost civility, was warm in his praise and sharp in his rebuke. And there had been no more invitations to the Greek Islands.

Felix was now coming diagonally across the grass to her, carrying a wicker basket.

'Very grand, isn't it?' he said, holding it up for her inspection. 'Provided by my hotel.'

'Was Rick going to share it with us?' she asked curi-ously.

'Oh, no. I was going to send Rick home after the row-ing session to keep his own woman company.'

Frances found nothing to say to this. 'Own woman' caused her heart to flutter, but she wasn't going to be silly. She was going to enjoy this unlooked-for outing in the holiday spirit it was offered.

'Do you know, I believe we could get down to that cove if we tried. The track looks fairly well used. Do you fancy going below or would you rather sit on the top?' Felix asked, studying the cliff face carefully.

'Oh, below, please. I intended making for the beach myself for an hour or so this afternoon.'

'Oh, did you!'

'But not to swim, only to sunbathe,' she assured him hastily.

They made their way down and found it well within their limits. The sand was clean and smooth and in the suntrap caused by the hollow of the cliffs the heat came up to hit them.

'Phew! I shall have to strip off,' Frances exclaimed, looking round for a suitable rock as she felt in the bag for her bikini.

'And I shall keep my eyes turned modestly the other way while I unpack our lunch,' said Felix, carrying the basket to the shade of another rock.

When she emerged a few minutes later, clad in her black bikini, Frances was determined not to feel self-conscious. It wasn't as if Felix hadn't seen her in it before, he had, on numerous occasions over the past weeks when they had all been to the beach, but that had always been with a crowd and somehow ...

She walked purposefully across the sand, feeling the heat striking the bottoms of her bare feet. She had put her hair up that morning on to the top of her head in a tiny, old-fashioned knot, and this she now crowned with a floppy sun-hat.

'This sun is fantastic, isn't it?' She dropped down, seeing that Felix must have had his swimming trunks on under his trousers, for he had also stripped off and was now lying on his side, propped up on an elbow.

'Did you know that the colour of that hat perfectly matches the colour of your eyes?' he remarked casually, passing her a glass of white wine.

'Yes, I did, actually,' admitted Frances, giving a smirk. 'Hey, this is cold!' she exclaimed, taking another sip, 'and what a feast! Turkey salad! They have done us proud.'

'The wine is cold because it's surrounded by ice,' he explained, passing her the food.

'Mmm ... am I glad I haven't got to walk all the way back after this!' She lifted a brow. 'You *will* give me a ride, won't you, Felix?'

'If you behave. How did you get here?'

'By lorry, tractor and Shanks's pony.' Frances saw him frown and said quickly : 'All perfectly safe and friendly.'

'All perfectly safe and friendly my eye!' he retorted rudely. 'You've been lucky up to now—one day you might not be. Have you any idea what a temptation you are, Fances, walking around in the briefest of shorts, a clingy vest ...'

'It's not a vest!' she burst out with a snort of laughter. 'It's a ...'

'I don't care what it's called, it's provocative! You're asking for trouble being on your own in remote places— anywhere, not just here. I wish you wouldn't do it.'

There was silence and she peeped at him through her lashes, a teasing comment already on her lips.

He's serious, she thought in surprise, the words stopping short. The realisation disturbed her. Had she been silly? His profile was etched against the background of sand as he gazed stonily out to sea. Really tanned now, the Cornish sun finishing off what the Mediterranean had started, he looked fit and strong. What chance would she have if someone with Felix's physique came along and ...

'The lorry driver was a pet,' she said softly, 'and he

showed me photographs of his children.'

'I'm sure he was ...' Felix began wearily.

'... and the tractor driver was a woman.'

He turned to look at her, a reluctant smile hovering round his mouth.

'I'd never accept a lift from a man in a car,' she persisted.

He raised a mocking brow. 'Not even a man in a Lancia?'

'Ah! A Lancia would be a temptation ... I'd have to size him up,' Frances declared. She chewed her bottom lip. 'I won't do it again, Felix, I promise.'

The tawny eyes narrowed and he took a slow drink before replying. 'Thank you, it will make my mind easier. I really don't feel like having more drama on my hands than I already have.'

She swallowed down an irrational sense of disappointment at the impersonal reply. 'I hope I may still ride my bicycle?' she asked, her voice letting him know in no uncertain terms that she wasn't going to relinquish that without a struggle.

'You may still ride your bicycle. Now, have you had enough to eat? More wine?'

She smiled and shook her head. 'No more, thanks, it's been delicious.' She helped to pack the basket away and then unfurled her towel and lay face up, liberally smearing herself with sun-oil and perching the sun-hat across her forehead, shielding eyes and nose.

'I'm going to wander over there to the rock pools,' said Felix, rising to his feet. 'If I find a crab I'll bring him over and introduce you to him.'

'You needn't bother,' said Frances, and heard him laugh softly.

'Don't lie in the sun for too long. You have a good tan, but your skin is so fair that you could still burn.'

His shadow darkened her eyelids for a moment and then passed away.

Frances lay basking in the sun for a while, thinking how extraordinary life was. Who would have supposed that she would be sharing a deserted beach with Felix today, when they had spent no leisure hours alone together for all these weeks? She sat up, seeking him among the rocks. The tide was coming in and soon their tiny sanctuary would be covered, the waves dashing against the rocks. She couldn't see him and assumed he had turned the corner of the headland.

She rolled over and unhooked the back of her bikini top. She didn't want to spoil her even tan with strap marks, they were such a nuisance professionally, and she could easily do it up when she heard Felix returning.

When a shadow crossed her face a few minutes later, Frances nearly jumped out of her skin, not to mention her bikini! Opening her eyes quickly she saw Felix looking down at her. She shut them again.

'Oh, it's you, you made me jump.' She was acutely conscious of her bare back and the fact that she couldn't move without showing more than she wanted to do. And Felix would know exactly how she felt, she thought crossly, knowing that her face was flushed and hoping he would think it was from the wine and sun combined and not old-fashioned embarrassment. She waited for him to move, lifting her lashes slightly only to see his feet still in the same position.

There was a scuffle of sand and Frances felt him kneel down beside her, the flesh of his leg scorching hers.

Her eyes opened wide. 'What ...?'

'I'll oil your back and legs for you, Frances,' said Felix, reaching for the bottle in her bag and unscrewing the top. 'You've forgotten to do it,' he reproved gently.

'Oh, well, it's difficult to do yourself ...' she began weakly.

'Exactly. Lie still,' he ordered, amusement in his voice. 'You'll have sand mixed in with it if you're not careful,' and then : 'Relax!'

Frances gritted her teeth and clamped her eyes shut again. The oil was cool on her hot skin and his hands were very soothing. Unbidden, the thought of Corfu came to her ... of promises and sun, the sea and the sand, and the wine beneath the moon ... and the magic of the Island ...

Felix knew exactly what he was doing, of course, as he always did, she thought lethargically. He was careful to keep within the bounds of decency, but only just, and every nerve quivered to his touch as hands, smooth and firm, moved over her body with hypnotic strokes.

His voice was above her. 'There, that will do, I think,' he said in a lazy drawl, and she could have thrown sand in his face, in fury at herself for being so dim-witted as to let him put his hands on her, and at Felix for taking advantage of the situation.

She didn't, of course. For one thing, throwing sand was childish, and for another, he was just as likely to throw it back, so she murmured : 'Thanks,' and heard him lie down on the sand a few feet away, and then there was silence between them.

She must have dozed, but it couldn't have been for long. The sun had moved round and they were both now in the shade of a tall rock. Carefully, keeping one eye on the sleeping form, Frances re-hooked her top and sat up, feeling woolly-headed.

Felix seemed soundly asleep. The tide was creeping higher and although she had no idea how long it would take to reach the cliffs they would have to move soon anyway, for the time was getting on. She would have to wake him.

It was the sea, endlessly washing back and forth over the flat sand, that gave her the idea.

She rose carefully to her feet and ran lightly down to the water line. Taking off the sun-hat, she scooped it into the sea and tiptoed back to the sleeping form. Tip of tongue peeping between lips, she held the hat high, allowing a few drops to trickle on to Felix's bare chest, and then either because she was so absorbed in watching his face and not what she was doing, or the material suddenly became waterlogged and porous, the whole contents jettisoned out and landed with a splash all over him.

The next few things happened within seconds. Frances stared aghast at what she had done, and Felix woke with a muttered exclamation, springing to his feet, taking in the scene in a flash.

'No, Felix, please! It was an accident, I promise you!' Frances begged, backing slowly, laughter bubbling away beneath the words, however serious she tried to make them.

'An accident, you vixen! Do you expect me to believe that?' he demanded, scooping up the wet hat and flinging it away. He stood before her, hands on hips, the water still dripping down his body. 'Well, we shall see who likes a wetting, shall we?' he added gently, beginning to advance slowly towards her, his body movement lazy, belying the latent fitness and strength.

'Felix, you wouldn't,' urged Frances, tentatively backing away. 'Felix, don't you dare!' she wailed, and turning, she ran.

She realised that she might just as well have stayed and accepted punishment there and then. The beach had shrunk in size owing to the incoming tide and she was laughing so much she could hardly run away.

She managed a crazy circle, shouting for mercy, before Felix caught her, scooping her up in his arms as if she weighed nothing, and marching down towards the sea, ignoring her struggles which were useless. There she was unceremoniously dropped.

The shock of the cold water against her warm body forced an involuntary screech from her lips and then all her energies were concentrated on revenge. Felix ran tantalisingly along the edge of the sea, just out of her reach, laughing, until he misjudged the surface beneath his feet and trod on a submerged stone. Taking advantage of his body being slightly off balance, Frances gave a good push and the next minute he too was under.

She didn't wait. He caught her half-way up the beach and they rolled on to the sand.

'I'm sorry, sorry, sorry,' Frances gasped, laughter dying as her wet body responded with tingling vitality to the weight of his own, pressed hard against her. 'You win,' she breathed, fighting for breath and composure, suddenly still.

Felix eased his weight. 'You look rather sandy, Miss Heron,' he observed.

'No more than you do, Mr Ravenscar,' she replied, equally grave.

He bent his head and kissed her gently, and the kiss tasted of salt, then he rose to his feet, pulled her up and together they ran down to the sea to wash away the sand.

Another half an hour of curiosity among the rock pools and they were dry, and viewing the rapidly encroaching sea, they decided to make tracks for home.

When Frances came back from changing, Felix was brushing the dry sand from his hair with his hands.

'I dread to think what mine looks like,' she said ruefully.

'It has a certain will-o'-the-wisp attraction,' conceded Felix, giving his lopsided grin.

'I'm sure it has,' she agreed, pushing her feet into sandals. 'Is that everything?'

'Not quite.'

Frances followed his gaze which had settled on her poor sun-hat, lying crumpled and forlorn where he had tossed it.

'It looks a wreck, but I'll take it,' she said with a laugh.

For sentimental reasons, she added to herself, picking it up and thrusting it into her bag, before giving a last look round the cove and following Felix up the cliff path.

CHAPTER SIX

WHEN her alarm rang at three the next morning Frances quietened it with her palm and gave a groan. It was still dark outside and her bed was very warm. Only the knowledge that Rick was calling for her in half an hour made her finally throw back the covers and tiptoe quietly to the bathroom.

She had warned the family at the farm that she would be rising early and had been given the freedom of the kitchen. Not that she could manage breakfast, even the thought of food made her feel queasy, but she did force a hot drink down before abandoning the warm kitchen. She was ready and waiting by the yard gate when Rick's headlights came sweeping round the bend and his van drew to a halt. She climbed in, trying to close the door noiselessly.

'Hullo, Rick. What a Godforsaken hour!'

He grinned. 'Wait until you see yon sunrise, then maybe you'll reckon it's worth it, lass,' he told her, swinging the vehicle round the narrow curving lanes, his headlights blazing a trail between the high hedgerows.

'If I can see it for the mist,' Frances grumbled, giving a yawn, 'and if I can keep my eyes open!'

'You'll be awake by the time we've finished with you,' Rick assured her with grim amusement, and Frances pulled a face.

'I know! I've read the script too, remember. This is the day I catch pneumonia,' she retorted, falling silent, wondering why she hadn't casually mentioned the day before that she had a horror of boats. Thinking of Felix and the unexpected time with him made her remember the apology that was owing and turning impulsively in her seat she said earnestly:

'Rick, I'm so sorry about yesterday, not turning up for rehearsal, I mean, but honestly, I wasn't given the message. Whatever dear Gemma says to the contrary, she didn't tell me. You know I'd own up if I'd just forgotten to come, don't you?'

He flicked her a glance and then returned his concentration to the road ahead. 'Aye, I ken that, lass, and it doesna' matter, we can start that bit earlier today ... it was really for you that Felix organised it.'

She nodded miserably. 'Yes, I know, that's what makes it worse.' She heaved a sigh. 'Oh, well, there's nothing can be done about it now.'

'And the day wasna' spoilt.'

Rick said this so blandly that Frances looked at him suspiciously. She couldn't tell whether he was referring to his day or her own.

'What did you do?' she asked at last.

'Och, I took the wife out for a wee bite to eat. And you?'

Frances pulled the duffle coat more warmly round her and pushed her hands deeply into the pockets. 'After a few unpleasant minutes we went for a picnic.' She stared out, not seeing the dark winding road ahead, but seeing instead a sun-drenched beach and two people laughing in the sand, suddenly silenced by a kiss.

'Well, the man had had a shock which wouldna' have

helped his nerves,' Rick observed, and Frances turned a puzzled face.

'What do you mean, a shock?' she asked.

Rick raised a brow. 'He didna' tell you, then? There was a lassie rescued by the lifeguard from the beach where we all meet, and rumour was flying round that it was you. It wasna' known if the lass had recovered or not. The boss went to the hospital and was told she'd died. He was asked to identify the body ... and was thankful to be able to tell them that it wasna' yourself.'

'Oh, Rick, how awful! I had no idea ... He never said a word,' Frances breathed, deeply distressed.

Rick could see how upset she was and purposely made her talk.

'What did you do after the picnic, then?'

'We played golf,' she told him. 'I used to play with my father in my early teens and I enjoyed playing a few holes again ... I suppose you never quite forget the basics.' She paused. 'Felix is good.'

'Aye, I would suppose he is. The boss likes to master whatever he sets out to do,' observed Rick with surprising insight.

'We finished up in a small pub, a lovely place, and Felix said that I sent the local blood pressure sky high with my shorts!' She grinned. 'They seemed to survive. I shall have to make my apologies to Julian when I see him. I had made a tentative arrangement with him for the evening.'

'He'll survive too,' was Rick's rather enigmatic reply.

Frances forced her thoughts away from the day before on to the day ahead. She brought out the script from her pocket, much folded and dog-eared, and by the light from the dashboard began to read it through. It was mostly action with very little dialogue, but it was the action part that was worrying her. Even the thought of it was enough to make her feel slightly sick. She told

herself crossly to pull herself together, that her imagination was exaggerating things out of all proportion, and
pushing the script back into her pocket she asked: 'Do
you think the sky is lighter, Rick?' and received a grunt
of assent in return.

He swung the van down towards the coast and after
a series of even narrower lanes, so narrow that had another vehicle approached it would have had to back up,
he finally turned off into a field, pulling up alongside the
row of studio trailers.

It was getting lighter all the time and technicians
were walking about, stamping their feet, talking quietly,
the red glow of an occasional cigarette or the chink of
a tea mug coming from the shadows.

Frances made her way to the trailer that housed the
costumes. Madge, the wardrobe mistress, was already
there, and without much conversation they began to
bring Mary Trewith once more to life, ready for the first
scene of the day's shooting.

As Madge helped her into a loosely woven green dress,
covered by a cream woollen shawl, she said: 'I've three
more dry changes for you, Frances. You're bound to get
soaked through, rehearsing this bit, and we'll save the
best dress and shawl for the final take.'

Frances nodded, smiled her thanks, rather tremul-
ously, and then left, working her way along the line until
she came to the make-up trailer. It was there she found
Julian, already in costume, and having the finishing
touches applied to his make-up. He turned as he heard
the door open.

'Come in, Frank, and close the door. No point in our
freezing to death before it's necessary. And stop looking
so agonised,' he admonished with mock severity. 'It's not
the first and probably won't be the last time I've been
stood up on a date.'

Frances pulled the door shut and sat herself down on

the chair next to his, switching on the overhead mirror light.

'I'm sorry, Julian, truly I am. Yesterday just did not go as planned.'

'Don't worry, dear girl,' Julian continued lightly, 'I had a very enjoyable chat with your farmer friend and tasted some of his excellent elder wine. When the message came that you were going to be late . . .'

'Message? What message?' demanded Frances, startled.

Julian waited while the make-up girl flicked the loose powder from his face before answering. 'The message that Felix phoned through to your farmer friend to say you were safe, not kidnapped or attacked, and would be late,' he explained patiently.

'I didn't know he'd done that,' Frances said slowly, remembering that Felix had made a phone call at the pub where they had stopped. The make-up girl draped a protective covering over her costume and began to tie her hair back. Frances caught Julian's pensive look through the mirror and pretended she hadn't.

With make-up completed it was only necessary for the hairdresser to do her job and then they were both walking along the cliff-top and down towards the shore. The technical crew were already there, dotted along the sand, some positioned up near the Morwenstow Church.

It was getting quite light now, but the breeze was sharp and the sea looked grey and uninviting. Felix was also there, talking to his crew, pointing to where the cameras were to be set. As Frances and Julian crunched over the shingle towards him Felix came to meet them. He was dressed in a short, warm coat, collar upturned, and his trousers were tucked into serviceable Wellington boots. He greeted them with a brief nod and went straight into the details of the filming.

'We have about an hour to rehearse and then the light

will be right, and with any luck, the tide too. You'll be over there, Julian,' and Felix turned, pointing out to sea at some rocks, only the tips of which were showing above the waves, 'and you'll be clinging for dear life. Frances will row over, help you into the boat and get you back to shore. Don't forget that your arm is supposed to be broken. I'm afraid it's going to be a cold, wet session for you both.' He swung round and peered at Frances. 'Are you all right?' he asked sharply, and when she nodded, continued briskly :

'Frances, you will then help Julian up the cliff path towards the church. We have a camera set just inside and you'll both enter by the main doors, which you, Frances, will shut behind you and turn the key.' He paused. 'Is that clear? Any questions?' When none were forthcoming, Felix walked down the beach.

Julian exchanged a wry look with Frances and putting his arm round her shoulders gave her a squeeze. She looked up and smiled gratefully. She had said nothing to Julian about her anxiety for the job ahead, but realised he must have sensed that she was not happy about what she had to do.

'Right, Frances, come and have a go,' came the call from the water's edge, and with a deep breath she clutched the shawl together and plodded stoically across the sand. When she reached him, Felix said :

'Mr Johnson's going with you this time, to make sure you know what you're doing, and then Rick will take his place with the camera. If you capsize, don't worry, we have two powerful motorboats at the ready to drag you out.'

'How reassuring,' commented Frances, willing her stomach not to disgrace her.

'You'll have to row alone for the long-distance shots,' he told her, swinging round to check again the camera angle, and then returning his regard to her, 'but by then you should be quite proficient at it—we hope! The tide will help you going out to the rocks, but it will be quite a pull coming back. If you can't manage it, we'll do a fake.'

Frances nodded and smiled weakly, and Felix began to lead her towards the boat.

'Cheer up. Kitchen's cooking a grand breakfast for when it's all over. In you get, let's get started.'

Frances splashed through the surf, the coldness of the water acting as an abrasive, and climbed awkwardly into the boat. The rowing part wasn't going to bother her, she had often gone out with her pals as a child and could handle oars as well as any boy. No, it was the memories that would come rushing back once she was out there where the swell was high ... and she shut off her thoughts and began to pull on the oars.

For the next two hours they all worked hard under extremely difficult conditions, but it was Frances and Julian who bore the brunt of the physical exertion. Three times they changed into dry clothes, forcing scalding hot drinks down for warmth. When the time came for the final take everyone was working with grim determination to get the job over and done with as quickly as possible. Working with senses heightened, their experience stretched to the utmost, so that the shots and the acting would be good, and precious time and energy wouldn't be wasted for any re-takes.

Rowing the boat across to the rocks, Frances had a momentary panic as it lifted high on the crest of a huge mound of sea and in the next moment sank into the trough of the next wave. The only thing that kept her going was Felix's approval.

They went through the action of the script and by the time they were staggering up the cliff path neither Julian nor Frances was having to act their physical distress. Once inside the church Julian fell into a heap on the floor, giving a very real account of a man who had been marooned on rocks half covered by sea, and Frances, as she leaned her weight against the wooden door and turned the key, had no need to act her fatigue. The cameras continued to turn for a few more seconds and then stopped.

The side door opened and Felix appeared.

'Good! Well done, both of you. You've really excelled yourselves this time. I think we're going to be lucky—Rick's hopeful, anyway, and he's usually found to be right.' He looked at the two drenched figures and cut short his eulogies, saying sharply: 'Where are those blankets? Quickly now,' and he himself wrapped one round Frances as she stood, teeth chattering, face pale, the water dripping into a puddle at her feet. 'Off you go, get changed and then breakfast.' He gave her a push to follow Julian who was already disappearing out of the church, and almost before she was out of the door she could hear him discussing the next scene with the cameramen.

Oh, well, that's his job, she told herself crossly, and if you expect him to come fussing over you then you're a bigger fool than I thought! Be thankful for his words of praise.

Shivering and forcing her limbs to obey her, she plodded along the rough path. It was going to be a nice day later. Down below on the beach she could see the dreaded rowing boat being pulled up out of the water. The rocks where they had enacted their drama were now high and dry and most innocuous-looking, but she could still feel the rise and fall of the boat beneath her, could still hear the slap of the waves against the staves.

Walking was becoming difficult, the heavy water-sodden material of her dress was clinging round her legs and the blanket was becoming a dead weight. She heard someone running up from behind and was thrust forward by an arm round her waist.

'Come on, girl, you'll be sneezing all over us if you don't get into something dry quickly!' It was Felix.

'I'm awfully wet, Felix, you'll get ...'

'Never mind me, get a move on,' he ordered, half dragging her along the cliff-top. The grass was wet with dew and a rabbit scampered not ten yards away. Frances, gritting her jaw together and concentrating on the dressing-room trailer in the distance, realised that she wasn't going to make it and couldn't hide her distress any longer.

'I'm sorry, but I'll have to ...' She broke away and began to retch, waves of nausea sweeping over her. She was aware that Felix was supporting her head and when she had finished a handkerchief found its way into her hand. She said shakily:

'I'm always borrowing your ...'

'What's wrong, Frances?' he demanded, concern making his voice brusque. 'I didn't think you looked well at the start, but you said you were all right.'

'I'm not ill,' she managed, trying to control the shaking.

'Like hell you're not,' he said grimly, lifting her protesting into his arms and striding across the field. 'You should have said something before,' he told her angrily, his breath warm on her face, 'we could have worked in someone to double up, the long-distance shots, anyway, or even put it off altogether for another day.' He set her on her feet and pushed open the trailer door, calling peremptorily: 'Madge!' and when Madge appeared, continued: 'Get her into some dry clothes as quick as you can, there's a dear,' and looking down at Frances, he added: 'I'll send someone over with a brandy ...'

'I don't like ...'

'... in five minutes!' and the door shut behind him.

Madge raised her brows and began to peel off the wet clothes.

Three-quarters of an hour later, feeling warmer, Frances was sipping strong hot tea, laced with brandy. She was on her own in the trailer and glad of it, for she wasn't in complete control, even yet. She gave a sigh and rested her chin thoughtfully on her hands.

Now it was all over she felt a great weariness sweeping over her, not merely physically but mentally as well. She had known the shooting of those scenes was not going to be easy, but the reality had been far worse than she had expected and the fact depressed her. The tensions of the morning welled up and turning her face to the cushion she gave way to tears, a measure of relief in the action.

She didn't really know what she was crying about, only knew the need to do so.

She didn't hear the door open, only felt the hand on her shoulder and she looked up, lashes wet and tears on her cheeks, to see Felix staring down at her. She sat up quickly, brushing her hand across her face and turning slightly away so that he couldn't see it.

'The message came that I wouldn't be needed yet,' she said gruffly, acutely embarrassed that he had found her in such a state.

'What's wrong, Frances?'

Had his voice been sympathetic she would have dissolved into tears again, but it was brisk and expressionless and was a douche to her spirits, making her reply crossly:

'Nothing's wrong! For goodness' sake, can't I have any peace? Go away and leave me alone! I'm all right!' and she willed him to go. She felt him sit down on the seat next to her.

'Don't be ridiculous. Of course something's wrong, and I'm certainly not leaving you like this. If you'd

sooner I sent for someone else to be with you, I will . . .'
and when she furiously shook her head, he continued:
'Have you had a row with Raynor because of yesterday? Is that why you're upset?'

She stiffened. 'Julian? No, of course not.'

'Then if it's not him, what are you crying about?'
Felix asked, and when she didn't answer, he added
roughly: 'For goodness' sake, Frances, I'm not an ogre!
You've climbed cliffs, ridden horses, done innumerable
difficult things and if you were worried you should have
told me today's work was too much for you and I would
have understood.'

'It wasn't,' she muttered. 'Oh, go away . . .'

'I'm not going until you tell me what's wrong . . .'

'All right, I'll tell you! You'll keep on and on if I
don't,' she cried, swinging round to face him, her tear-
stained face white with emotion. 'My parents were
drowned in the sea off this coast . . . our boat capsized
and I was the only one of us saved. Now do you understand? We were in the water for ages, clinging to the
side of the boat, and when my mother finally slipped
under my father tried to save her and then there was
just me! The rescue boat came too late!' Her face
crumpled and she turned into the cushion again but was
pulled on to his chest. 'I know it's stupid of me,' she
gasped out, 'and I'm not usually s–so silly . . .'

After a moment Felix said quietly:

'Why didn't you tell me how you felt? I'm beginning
to think that perhaps I am an ogre.'

'No, you're not,' Frances said wearily, sitting up and
wiping her face, 'and I didn't tell you because ten years
is a long time and I thought . . . I hoped I'd forgotten
what it was like.' She shrugged and attempted a smile.
'I hadn't. If we'd had that scene scheduled for the beginning of shooting perhaps it would have been different.
I've known it was there to be done eventually, looming

nearer and nearer, and it probably got out of all proportion. Anyway, early or late, what good would it have done—telling you, I mean? The work had to be done.' She blew her nose and chanced a look at his face. It was rather bleak and her heart sank. 'I'm sorry, Felix, I don't often get the blues.'

He stood up and crossed to the door. 'Do you feel up to carrying on working today?'

'Of course I do,' she replied, appalled at the question. 'I feel much better now, honestly. The brandy and the cry has done the trick.' She waited for him to smile in return, but waited in vain, and she ended up by repeating: 'I'd rather work, please.'

'Very well.' He looked at her thoughtfully. 'What am I going to do about you, Frances?' he asked after a long pause.

She bit her lip. 'I don't know, Felix. You'll be rid of me altogether after this week and then the thorn will be removed from your flesh.' Even that received no response and she finished weakly: 'I'm sorry I'm such a nuisance to you.'

He gave her another searching look and left the trailer without answering.

The weather changed at the end of the week, but by then all the film was in. Word had come back from London over the week that the studio was pleased with the high quality of film already sent in for processing, and Felix himself was satisfied with the way things had gone, according to Rick.

On the final Saturday before the mass exodus back to London, spirits were high as they celebrated the end of their hard work by a special dinner dance at one of the exclusive country clubs in the district.

Frances wore a cream dress which showed off her tan to perfection. She knew she looked good, but she could have been dressed in sackcloth for all the impression it made on the one person she wanted to impress. Felix was charming and polite but didn't ask her to dance once, and she was more than grateful for Julian's presence, although she felt bad about using him in such a way. When she at last crawled into bed, worn out with trying to look happy, she decided it was a good job the work was finished ... and she could put Felix right out of her life.

Julian took her back to London the next day, the Panther eating up the miles and performing like the stalwart she was. When the time came to say goodbye he looked at her thoughtfully and said:

'We've had some fun, haven't we, Frank?'

She nodded and they stood for a moment, her head resting on his shoulder, before she murmured:

'Thank you for being so sweet, Julian. I'll never forget you.'

He lifted her chin and planted a kiss on the end of her nose.

'Who knows, we may be getting together for another seven instalments,' he said lightly, and then, as if his words had only just struck him, he pulled a face, adding quickly: 'Not yet, though, I want to get back into the theatre for a spell, the stage is my true love.'

'Mmm ... me too, I think,' Frances agreed.

'And what do you think of Black Felix, now that you've worked for him?'

She found herself flushing slightly beneath his keen scrutiny, and replied carefully: 'I think he's an extremely good director. I wouldn't have missed working for him for anything.' She smiled and said gently: 'I'm all right, Julian, honestly.'

'Good.' He kissed her on the lips briefly. 'Take care, Frank. Keep in touch,' and almost before she could say: 'Goodbye, Julian,' he had gone.

Zoe naturally was glad to have her back, the flat had

been like a morgue, so she informed Frances, and for the first full day together they didn't seem to stop talking.

'By the way, Frankie, your Doctor Williams rang up last week to see if you were back,' stated Zoe, bringing in two plates of curried beef and rice and placing them on the table.

'Oh, did he? And he's not my Doctor Williams,' replied Frances, sniffing the food appreciatively. 'Mmm ... this smells good, Zoe.'

'Yes, it does, rather,' agreed Zoe complacently, returning after a few mouthfuls to her original theme. 'He came to see the show and took me out for a drink afterwards. He's rather sweet, isn't he? Think how useful it would be to be married to a doctor, Frankie. He'd be right there, on the spot, if you had a pain in your big toe!'

'He's a heart specialist, Zoe,' Frances replied vaguely. Talking about Cornwall had brought it all back to her and the future was looking bleak.

'I know that, idiot, but he must know something about toes as well as hearts! Stop being so pedantic and deliberately obtuse—I was trying to be funny! Frankie, he must have been interested to have rung you up after all these weeks,' Zoe persisted, but gaining no response, she gave up.

Trying to forget certain aspects of the past weeks was not made any easier by the fact that Lady Ravenscar seemed determined not to lose touch. A week after returning to London, Frances received a summons to take tea.

Lady Ravenscar was quite happy to talk about her son, and Frances found that she was quite happy to listen. Felix did not put in a surprise appearance ... Frances hadn't expected him to, but was weak enough to hope.

When he telephoned mid-week she could hardly believe it. When the conventional pleasantries had been dealt with, Felix continued:

'Mother has asked me to ring to see if you're free next Saturday evening. My sister Jessica, with her husband, is paying us a flying visit and Mother would like you to meet her. It will be a small, informal affair—can you make it?'

Frances hesitated, but only momentarily. She knew she ought to make some excuse and still found herself calmly accepting. 'Is she younger than you, Felix, this sister of yours?' she asked curiously.

There was a note of surprise in his voice. 'She's my twin. I thought you knew that.'

'Goodness, no, I didn't! Your mother has never mentioned it, but she probably thought you had. How exciting, being a twin!' she enthused, trying to imagine what Jessica would look like and failing abysmally.

'It has its drawbacks,' his voice came over dryly. 'I'll pick you up around seven. Until then . . .'

Frances replaced the receiver after saying goodbye and wandered over to the window, trying to analyse her feelings. She should have made some excuse. Brief, tantalising meetings were not going to help her get over this ridiculous . . . she struggled for the right word and came up with involvement as being the one nearest to what she was prepared to admit . . . for Felix Ravenscar. She turned away with an exasperated exclamation and began to prowl the apartment, telling herself crossly that she would go this time, she would allow herself this one meeting, and then no more. Felix had made it perfectly plain in what capacity she could fill his life and it was up to her either to take what little he could offer, or leave well alone. Somewhere hovering in the middle wasn't going to satisfy either of them.

When the bell rang just after six on the Saturday

evening, Frances stared at the clock in surprise. If this
was Felix then he was very early. Hurrying to the door
she opened it, a greeting on her lips, a greeting which
was cut off as she looked at the man standing on the
landing, a hesitant half-smile on his face and a slightly
anxious look in his brown eyes.

'Hullo, Frances.'

'Mark!' She could hardly believe her eyes. 'Why, Mark
Lucas, what on earth ...?' She pulled herself together
and smiled, reaching out to take his hand, drawing him
inside. 'Mark, how nice to see you, come in. How well
you're looking. Let me take your coat ... sit down.' She
knew she was talking too much, but she couldn't get
over her surprise at seeing him—Chichester and Mark
seemed many moons ago.

Mark was studying her closely as he seated himself.
'You haven't changed, Frances,' he observed with a
smile. 'Maybe even a little more beautiful than you were
a year ago—and just as kind ... I thought you might
have shut the door in my face.'

Frances said gently: 'You should know I wouldn't do
that, Mark. How are you? I read some good reviews on
your Edinburgh season. Are you enjoying doing the
classics for a change?'

He nodded. 'It has been most satisfying. Going there
was the best thing I could have done, for more reasons
than the job.' He hesitated. 'You're not cross that I came
to see you, Frances?'

'Of course not.'

Mark leaned forward restlessly. 'I came because I
wanted to satisfy myself that you were well, and that I
hadn't completely ruined your career. Are you happy,
Frances?' and he searched her face intently, looking for
the truth in her eyes.

Frances found herself releasing a long breath of relief.
Everything was going to be all right.

'I'm fine, Mark, truly. I've been working steadily since Chichester, just finished a television series, as a matter of fact, and there's the chance of a Shaw revival at Leeds.' She smiled reassuringly. 'You don't have to worry about me.'

'I can't tell you what that means, to hear you say that.' Mark took out a cigarette case and offered her one.

'No, thanks.' Frances paused and then asked: 'How's Midge?'

He lit his cigarette before speaking. 'Midge is fine,' he told her, crossing to the table for an ashtray. 'Now that she has a certain amount of choice and can work free-lance, she's able to stay wherever I am. A fashion house in Paris is taking her designs regularly now, so Midge is well and happy.' He gave a short laugh and scratched the back of his head thoughtfully. 'Actually, she's pregnant and over the moon with excitement—you'd think no one had ever had a baby before!'

'Oh, Mark, I am pleased!' Frances said warmly. 'Congratulations.'

He gave a rueful smile. 'I was past thinking of myself as a parent, and can't begin to imagine myself as one, even now.'

'Nonsense, you'll make a wonderful father,' she said firmly. 'When is the baby due?'

He grinned broadly. 'In the New Year ... we've only just had it confirmed, so we've enough time to get used to the idea.' He drew on the cigarette, his face serious again. 'I have a lot to thank you for, Frances ... you've been on my conscience.'

'Well, you can just wipe me off it,' Frances said crisply. 'Stop feeling guilty about me, Mark, it's unnecessary. As you can see, I'm well and happy. What happened at Chichester between us wasn't based on reality, was it? We were both lonely and our emotions were stretched tight because of the play. I promise to look back on our time there with only fond memories. No bitterness, honestly.'

'Bless you, Frances,' Mark smiled, taking her hand in his and holding it for a moment. 'I'd better go.' He picked up his jacket and Frances walked slowly with him to the door. 'Do you still share with that mad friend of yours, Zoe?'

Frances laughed at the description. 'Yes—and that reminds me, I promised I'd post a letter for her. I'll come down with you and pop it in the box on the corner,' and collecting the envelope from the mantelpiece she rejoined him and together they made their way down the stairs. As they emerged into the early evening sunshine Frances said in surprise: 'Is this your car, Mark? You have a new one?'

He nodded, searching for the keys in his pocket. Looking at the distinctive coloured Citroën, Frances added teasingly: 'I wouldn't have thought red to be quite you, somehow.'

Mark pulled a wry smile, unlocking the door. 'Midge chose it.' He stood looking at her for a moment, putting his hands on her shoulders, head tilted consideringly. 'When you opened the door to me just now you looked like a girl who was expecting someone special. Were you, Frances?'

She found herself nodding. It would do Mark good to think she was in love . . . and she supposed, in a way, that Felix was someone special. Mark leaned forward and brushed his lips across her mouth.

'Goodbye, Frances, my dear. I wish you all the best. He's a lucky fellow, but he must know that already. Take care.'

'Goodbye, Mark, and the best of luck to you and Midge.'

He smiled and climbed into the car, raising his hand in a brief salute as he accelerated away. Frances stood for a few seconds watching the Citroën out of sight, before walking on to the corner. She slipped Zoe's letter into the postbox and returned, thinking deeply. She was glad Mark had come. It had been a closing of a chapter, for her as well as for him. Looking at him now it seemed hard to believe the heart-searchings of a year ago.

She ran up the stairs, feeling light-hearted, realising with mild panic that time was pressing on. She had barely been in for more than a few minutes when the bell went.

Giving an exasperated groan, Frances grabbed the dressing gown from off the back of the bathroom door, switched off the shower, thankful that she hadn't actually stepped under it, and padded once more to the front door.

For the second time in less than an hour the greeting on her lips faltered. It *was* Felix this time, but his face gave no encouragement for the words she had ready.

'Hullo, Felix.' Frances held the door wide and he stepped past and carried on into the living room. She closed the door, a slight frown creasing her forehead, and followed him, tying the belt of her gown as she went. 'I'm sorry I'm not ready. Won't you sit down? Would you like to help yourself to a drink, I won't be long.' His silence was unnerving and she looked at him uncertainly.

'I'd rather stand, thank you.' His long searching scrutiny brought a faint colour to her cheeks.

'Is something wrong, Felix?' A flicker of alarm stirred in her breast and her hand came up to hold the folds of the gown at her throat. 'Why do you look at me like that?'

'I'm trying to see what it is about you that makes a normally sensible and intelligent man behave contrary to expectations.'

His voice was very controlled, but she could tell that

he was angry, and the intensity of his anger was almost tangible. Her eyes wide, she searched his face in bewilderment.

'I don't understand ...' she faltered, and he cut in swiftly:

'It's quite obvious that you don't, or else you wouldn't have let Mark Lucas come anywhere near you while I was around! Quite a poignant little scene I've been witnessing. Has this been going on ever since Chichester?' When shock rendered her speechless, he spat out: 'Well, has it? Answer me!'

'I ...' She swallowed. 'You know Mark?' she whispered incredulously.

'I should do. He's married to my sister Jessica!' He looked at her stunned face. 'Quite a coincidence, isn't it? That makes him my brother-in-law,' he added facetiously.

A wave of colour swept over her face and then went, leaving it ashen. She put a hand to her forehead. 'I ... I can explain, Felix.'

He gave a short, hard laugh. 'I'm sure you can, but I don't need explanations, thank you, I have the evidence of my own eyes.' He turned away as if the sight of her was more than he could bear, and hands gripping the edge of the table, exclaimed with contempt in his voice: 'For God's sake stop acting the innocent! I know all about you and Mark at Chichester, have known ever since you said your name to Tom Deverell at the audition, so don't insult my intelligence, please. You've already played out your game of comedy where I'm concerned—and had me believing you, damn you!'

Frances dropped her hand to her side, saying quietly: 'I wouldn't have thought even you to be so quick to jump to conclusions, Felix. Any number of innocent explanations could be put to what you've just seen ...'

'And I'm sure you could furnish me with them all,

and do each one convincingly!' His voice made her flinch as he swung round on her. 'I've never denied that you're an excellent actress, Frances, but even I under-estimated your capabilities.'

Her limbs began to tremble and she clutched the back of a chair for support, lifting her chin proudly as she said: 'Judge, jury and executioner? How arrogant of you, Felix! But then my first opinion was that no man should be so sure of himself as you are.'

She couldn't believe that this was happening. She wanted him to go out and ring the bell and let them both start again ... but this charade was to be played out to the last word, and had begun long before they had met. She made another effort and despised herself for the note of pleading in her voice.

'Felix, I don't know how much you know, but it's not what you think, honestly ...'

'No? Can you deny that Mark Lucas was willing to leave his wife because he'd formed an attachment with you?' Felix waited. 'Well? Can you?'

She could not deny it, of course, and her face told him so.

'Midge,' Frances said faintly, grasping at straws. 'Mark calls his wife Midge.'

'A nickname. I can assure you there's no mistake. Mark Lucas, aged thirty-eight, professional actor, fair hair and brown eyes, good voice, now working in Edin-burgh but previously in Chichester.' He reeled off the information in a hard, flat voice. 'Mark Lucas with whom you enacted that tender love scene a few moments ago, and many more at Chichester, I have no doubt!' He strode towards her and his hands grasped her upper arms. 'I don't know how you've managed to en-tice him back into seeing you again, but you won't keep him. Mark's always wanted a family. I believe, in the long run, you'll find you come a very poor second. A of stuff on the side is always a precarious part to play.'

'I hardly think you are qualified to show sanctimonious outrage, Felix,' Frances ground out between clenched teeth. Anger was her only weapon against such biting scorn. It cut through the numbness and leaden ache that had descended upon her.

'I don't play around with married women. I keep to the rules and no one gets hurt.'

She almost laughed aloud. No one gets hurt! She wrenched herself away and ran towards the bathroom door. In a few strides he had cut her off.

'Where the hell do you think you're going?' Felix demanded savagely.

'Anywhere away from you,' she returned wildly. 'Close the door behind you when you go out!'

'I haven't finished with you yet. You're staying right here.' Their eyes locked in a battle of wills. 'Even if I have to use force,' he added grimly.

Frances glared, chest rising and falling rapidly, chin high and cheeks bright red with rage. 'I can quite believe that! God Almighty Felix Ravenscar must have his say! Very well, as I have no choice in the matter I'll stay, but I'll never forgive you, Felix. You'll regret this day and when you leave I never want to see you again in my life!' She swung round and abruptly seated herself. 'Well?'

Felix stared at her and then walked to the window to stand frowning out for a few moments. 'How often have you been seeing him?' he demanded at last, turning to face her.

She raised her brows. 'Why don't you ask Mark?' she taunted. 'Or doesn't he know that dear brother-in-law is keeping tabs on him?' She watched with pleasure his face darken and a nerve jump in his cheek. 'No, of course he doesn't know,' she added scornfully.

'I wouldn't need to ask the question, would I? So far

as I was concerned the affair between you was finished
when he went to Edinburgh, and Jess joined him there.'

Frances leaned forward, eyes widening. 'It was you!
You got him that job!' She gave a short laugh. 'That's another thing I don't suppose Mark's going to be very
pleased about.' She gave an eloquent shrug. 'What are
you going to do now? Smack his bottom and tell him to
be a good boy and run home to wifey? What a dutiful
brother wifey has!' and her voice was full of sarcastic
wonderment.

There was an ominous silence, and then: 'Jessica
doesn't know about you and won't know, unless you
force my hand. Regarding Chichester, I merely made
enquiries. If you thought you were being discreet I'm
sorry to disappoint you. I baited the Edinburgh hook,
certainly, though he need not have snapped at it ... but
actors tend to be ruthless where their careers are concerned, and I made sure the bait was a juicy one.'

Frances turned her face away and drew a hand over
her eyes. She could, she supposed, tell him now that it
was she who had left Chichester first, but what was the
point? He wouldn't in all probability believe her. The
only person who perhaps he would believe was Mark,
and even then it wasn't certain, and she couldn't do that
to Mark. She couldn't hurt his pride or his new-found
happiness by bringing the whole business of Felix's involvement to light. And did it matter what Felix Ravenscar thought of her? She was nothing to him ... and he
was nothing to her!

She lifted her head and said steadily: 'How do you
expect to stop Mark from seeing me, Felix? I'm most
intrigued.'

Felix looked coldly at her. 'I have no intention of
stopping him. I'm not a fool. If Mark's weak enough to
keep on with this affair then Jessica is better off without
him ... rather than share him with a two-faced bitch

like you.' He smiled. 'You don't like that, do you, Frances? Well, I'm afraid the "other woman" has to put up with such labels however much they offend her sense of dignity.' He shrugged. 'But I believe Mark is really in love with Jess and only infatuated with you, and once the child comes ...' He allowed the unfinished sentence to speak for itself, adding slowly : 'Now that you know your little game is out in the open, to me at least, you might consider Mark is not worth it.'

Frances looked at him sharply. 'And just what do you mean by that? It sounds very much like a threat.'

He gave a thin smile. 'It's only a threat if you're not sensible. If I find that you do anything silly, like obtaining work where Mark is, then I shall make life very difficult for you professionally. Your future could be limited.' He raised his brows. 'You hadn't thought of that? How naïve of you!'

Frances thrust herself from the chair, arms clasped round her body as if she were cold. Moving to the mantelpiece she took a cigarette from the box and lit it with trembling hands. She rarely smoked, but had she not done something at that moment she would have hit him—and in the state he was in, he would surely have hit her back, she had no illusions about Felix Ravenscar.

'Thank you for warning me.' She inhaled slowly, trying for composure. 'I suppose that was why you were so angry, the night of your mother's birthday? You thought I was worming my way into the family circle because of Mark! It must have been a relief when you realised that I didn't know the connection. I must say you covered up very well, but you're something of an actor yourself, aren't you, Felix?' She gave a short, bitter laugh. 'Everything is beginning to make sense now. I always knew there was a reservation ...'

'And you almost had me fooled. I began to think that my informant had got Chichester all wrong,' Felix said impatiently. 'Shows what a clever girl you are, doesn't it?'

'It must do, to almost fool the experienced Felix Ravenscar,' retorted Frances, stubbing out her cigarette. 'I'm glad I had the chance, it was quite amusing at times.' She thought she had gone too far and hurried on quickly: 'I think you'd better go now. You've had your say.'

'I'll go when I'm ready, and not before,' he announced grimly, and moved to stand a yard away, hands on hips, stance quietly menacing. 'Naturally we shall not expect you this evening, or any other evening. I'll make your abject apologies to my mother and you'll fade out of her life, do you understand? Any gratitude we felt about the way you helped her is now wiped clean. Allowable, I think you'll agree, when you realise that you are a threat to her daughter and unborn grandchild. I shouldn't like to have to tell her the sort of person you really are, but I shall do so if you force my hand.'

This was too much! Frances had come to care and respect Lady Ravenscar ...

'You know *nothing* about me, Felix, nothing!' she burst out passionately, her face white with anguish. 'In your arrogance you think you do, but you don't!'

'I know you're a very beautiful and dangerous woman ...' he responded savagely, pulling her roughly to him and bringing his mouth down on hers.

When Frances was able to wrench her mouth away, she gasped: 'Damn you, Felix, let me go or I'll ...'

'That act you put on about Corfu was quite impressive ...'

'That rankles, doesn't it?' she ground out in rage, struggling ineffectively to free herself. 'The fact that I didn't jump at the chance of being your latest paramour must have been a shock to your inflated ego! Let me tell you, Felix, that ...'

'I'm sure Mark wouldn't mind sharing, if that's what's worrying you.'

She wrenched a hand free and brought the palm across the side of his face with a stinging slap. All movement was suspended.

Their eyes held and then Felix smiled and when he spoke his voice was lazily insolent.

'I still find you desirable, and you feel the same way about me, whatever else you may say, my dear Frances.'

'I feel only loathing for you,' she whispered, tears of helpless anger glistening on her lashes.

He let her go. 'I expect you do. No one likes being found out, do they? Just remember what I've said, for your own sake.'

'Remember?' She gave a harsh laugh. 'Don't worry, I shall never forget what you've said, Felix, never.' Her eyes flashed as she added grimly. 'It's dangerous to play God, Felix ... one day you'll find that out.'

Tawny eyes held blue ones and then Felix turned on his heel and left, the front door marking the finality of it all by shutting with a decisive bang.

CHAPTER SEVEN

THE antidote to unhappiness often lies in work, and Frances threw herself into the rehearsals with grim determination. The initial weeks in Leeds were hard, so that at the end of the day she was so tired she didn't have the energy to lie awake brooding. Gradually she regained her balance, told herself that she truly did not care what Felix thought of her, made new friends, and the wretched 'Ravenscar affair', as she found herself calling it, began to recede.

Frances was asked to stay on and she accepted with alacrity. The longer she could remain away from London the better.

Forwarded mail brought newsy letters from Zoe, whose play was now into its second year. There was also an occasional letter from Lady Ravenscar. Frances replied in her usual friendly way, leaving the period between answering a little longer each time, hoping to be able to disappear out of the scene eventually. She had no intention of accepting Lady Ravenscar's repeated invitations to visit when she returned to London, and knew that she could only end up being a disappointment, but there was nothing she could do about that.

In the middle of October *Penruth* was screened on the television, giving Frances a certain amount of notoriety among the company at Leeds. A photograph of Felix appeared advertising the serial, together with one or two of the cast, her own ironically adjoining his.

That won't please him, Frances thought with grim humour, as she read the written interview below, her eyes going back to the photograph, so familiar to her, remembering how many times she had suppressed the urge to smooth away the tiny frown that sometimes creased his brow. Felix Ravenscar, so the caption told her, was at the moment working on a documentary programme about the people living on the island of Mull.

You can be in Timbuktu for all I care, she told the photograph bitterly.

For she was still embittered, still deeply hurt by the harsh accusations that had been hurled at her. Admittedly, as the weeks passed, their angry final meeting faded slightly and she became more philosophical about it all. Certainly the success of *Penruth* in some measure made up for the heartache. *Something* constructive had come out of their association.

Frances returned to London prior to Christmas, realis-

ing by the warmth of her feelings at the sight of the
decorations and gaily lit shops just how glad she was to
be back.

Penruth brought in gratifying offers of work, both
from the theatre and television, and after careful consideration Frances accepted the part in a modern play,
written especially for television by an experienced
writer, and enjoyed minor praise from the critics when
it was screened early in February.

During the six months since her break with Felix,
Frances had been out with a number of men, but none
had stirred more than friendship in her. Not for the want
of trying, on both sides. More than anything, Frances
wanted to throw herself into a love affair, just to show
herself—what, exactly, she couldn't say ... or wouldn't
admit. And so a grand passion did not materialise. However much she willed it to, something always stopped
her from becoming committed each time.

It was no surprise, therefore, when the producer of
her latest play invited her to join him to attend a
luncheon in honour of a well-known actor who was
celebrating sixty years on the professional stage.

Knowing that she would be surrounded by representatives of all forms of entertainment, Frances looked
round her with interest as she followed her escort into
the banqueting hall of an exclusive London hotel. She
recognised many famous faces already seated at the
long tables covered with crisp white cloths and resplen-
dently set with glass and silverware.

As she took her place at one of them, the gentlemen
already there rising politely to their feet as she seated
herself, one particular face stood out among all the
strange ones.

Felix Ravenscar.

Frances stared, the colour coming and going in her
cheeks, and her heart missed a beat as he gave a slight

smile and leaned forward to take her hand.

'Hullo, Frances. How are you?'

Frances supposed she should be grateful to him for making an effort. After all, sitting with people who knew that they had worked together making *Penruth*, it would have been decidedly odd had he ignored her completely!

She managed a smile in return and murmured a greeting, and then to her relief the luncheon began. The food was delicious, but her appetite had gone, so had all her excited anticipation of the event. Why should you let Felix Ravenscar spoil things? she asked herself crossly. Ignore him! Forget him! But it was impossible for her to do so. The official speeches were amusing and in any other situation Frances would have been delighted, but she could not disassociate herself from the man sitting only a few yards away.

If she turned her head slightly she could see his hand, touching the stem of his wine glass, could see his dark head as he leaned forward as he laughed at some witticism, could hear his voice, beautiful and resonant, and all the old bitterness welled up inside her.

Frances fumed inwardly at the ill-luck that out of all the tables in the huge hall she should be placed at the same one as his! But any idea that it was a coincidence was soon dispelled by her escort, who turned to her at the end of the proceedings and said:

'If it wasn't for the fact that I owe Ravenscar a favour I should not be abandoning you to him now, believe me!' He rose and smiled down at her, curiosity alive in his eyes. 'He was most insistent that I should disappear at the first convenient opportunity, but I want you to know that I'm doing so with reluctance.'

Frances, the colour rising in her cheeks, said incoherently:

'There's no need, surely, for you to go ...' and stopped when she saw her escort's raised brows.

'My dear girl, Ravenscar's not a man to treat lightly, you know. You've worked with him once and it's obvious he's interested in using you again. Take advantage of the opportunity—and good luck!' and although greatly intrigued by the lengths to which Felix Ravenscar had engineered this meeting, he placed a hand briefly on her shoulder and then made his way across the hall to mingle with a group of guests just leaving.

Their table was now almost empty, the only other occupants being at the far end, and Frances turned to face him.

'I don't understand any of this,' she told him stonily.

'I know you don't. May I ...'

'Had I known it was at your instigation I wouldn't have come.'

'I know that too, hence the subterfuge. You won't have wasted your time, however. To be sitting at the same table as four established directors, two eminent actors and a playwright can't do you any harm ... and the food was good and the speeches amusing.' His voice was all reasonableness.

'Agreed, and I could perhaps have enjoyed the occasion under different circumstances,' she informed him bitterly.

Felix shrugged. 'That, I suppose, was inevitable.'

Frances stared at him. The man's composure was unbelievable! He could remember their last angry meeting and 'suppose' she found his company objectionable! And the fact that she had been manipulated into this meeting gave her a feeling of growing unease and helplessness. Such was Felix Ravenscar's position in her profession that he had a way of making things happen; he seemed even more invincible than ever, viewed after six months' absence. She sustained a swift measure of panic. Had she any control over herself or her destiny where Felix was concerned? The thought was so alarming that she took a sharp, inward breath, and told herself not to be such an idiot. She turned to pick up her clutch bag to give herself time to calm down, but she was still aware of him, standing by her chair, and every nerve tingled at his nearness, every facet of emotion passed fleetingly through her.

'You're at liberty to leave, of course, but I hope you'll give me a few moments,' and standing aside, Felix watched her steadily as she rose to her feet.

'Oh, I'll stay. I'm curious to know what it is that's made you go to such lengths,' Frances retorted, and allowed herself to be led to the comparative seclusion of one of the adjacent lounges where they seated themselves, Felix with his back partly turned to the rest of the room. Blocking her way out? Frances wondered, with grim amusement.

'I understand that Gareth has been seeing something of your apartment mate,' he said, by way of opening the conversation between them.

'Zoe? Why, yes, I believe he has,' agreed Frances, and looking at him sharply, added: 'Zoe is one of the best people I know and Gareth will come to no harm from her.'

Felix quirked a brow and replied evenly: 'You're very quick to take up arms on behalf of your friend. My question was quite innocent, I assure you, and anyway, Gareth is old enough to take care of himself.'

'Really? I'm amazed you should say that—with your habit of interfering in other people's lives!' she came back sarcastically.

His lips grimaced, but he ignored the implication, merely pulled his chair round slightly to accommodate a waiter who now arrived with a tray laden with coffee things.

There was silence as this was poured out, and when the waiter left, Frances said abruptly: 'Why have you arranged this meeting, Felix?'

'Because I knew that had I phoned, or called, you would have refused to speak or see me.'

'So you contrived a situation where I was forced to speak to you. Yes, I understand all that, it has the Ravenscar touch!' she answered decisively. 'But that's not what I meant. Why do you want to speak to me at all? Didn't you say enough the last time we met? It seemed pretty conclusive to me!'

He stirred his coffee thoughtfully. 'Yes, I was quite eloquent, wasn't I? Whereas you didn't say enough.' He waited a moment. 'You know as well as I do why I want to speak to you, Frances. I want to apologise to you for that last meeting.'

Of course, he was right—there could be only one reason. During all this time it was conceivable that he should stumble across the truth and find out how wrong he had been in his assumption that she was having an affair with his brother-in-law. How many times had she enacted this scene of apology in her imagination? Had thought with relish of the exultation she would feel!

And now it was actually happening ... and she felt nothing ... merely a curious anticlimax, a flatness as if all feeling had completely left her. She could even view dispassionately that the apology was typical of him—controlled and almost expressionless.

'And I'm to swoon with thankfulness, I suppose?' she asked at last. She lifted her eyes to his face and saw an unexpected pallor round his mouth. No, she thought, he's not used to apologising and doesn't like it.

'You have every right to be scathing,' he said slowly, 'although knowing your strong sense of justice I'm sure you'll grant that I had some justification in thinking what I did.'

She shook her head wonderingly and gave a laugh. 'Isn't it fine! Two seconds of your apology and you're saying it wasn't your fault!'

'That wasn't quite what I said, but you have a point.' Felix pushed away his cup and felt in his pocket, bringing out a case and lighter. He offered her a cigarette which she refused, and taking one for himself, he lighted it, his eyes upon her face. Drawing deeply on the cigarette and looking at her through the smoke, he added: 'I was angry that night, as angry as I've been for a long while, and said things that must have distressed you deeply.'

'Two-faced bitch?' suggested Frances.

'Yes, well, at the time, things seemed to be in favour of such a label. I'm sorry. As I say, I was angry, and because generally I'm under control, when I do unleash things tend to happen. I'm not proud of myself.' He stretched out a hand for an ashtray from the next table. 'Aren't you interested in why I should now have this volte-face?'

Frances lifted a shoulder. 'I suppose you've spoken to Mark.'

He ignored her uninterested voice and continued factually:

'I journeyed into Scotland last week to make the acquaintance of my new nephew—two weeks early and causing panic and confusion all round. Mark and I went out to celebrate the baby's arrival and as the whisky flowed so did Mark's confidences. He became garrulous and retrospective, and although I didn't consciously encourage him, I didn't stop him either, especially when he came to the relevant parts so far as you were concerned. He talked of many things during our alcoholic orgy, and rather naturally, because Chichester was really the turning point for both Mark and Jessica, that came up among a welter of reminiscences.' Felix paused for a moment, as if marshalling his thoughts. 'To understand fully I shall have to explain my relationship with my twin. I've always felt a responsibility towards Jessica. I've dragged her out of innumerable scrapes and I suppose she's come to rely on me too much in that way, hence her cry for help when things between her and Mark became sticky— I didn't want to interfere, I value Mark's friendship too much, but the ties of twinship were too strong.' He lifted his hands expressively. 'Jessica is intelligent and amusing, capable of deep feeling, but I'm afraid we Scorpions tend to like our own way. Now that's all right if you're answerable only to yourself, but when Jess married Mark she had to adjust and didn't find it easy.' He ground out his unfinished cigarette and frowned down at his hands, held loosely before him, elbows resting on his knees.

'I've known Mark for so many years, long before he and Jess met, that I suppose he felt he could tell me things that a brother-in-law would normally keep to himself— and he knows I haven't always approved of Jessica's actions. The most important thing that came out of his ramblings, so far as I was concerned, was that you left Chichester before he did, more or less encouraging him to give his marriage another chance.'

'How did my name come into things?' Frances felt compelled to ask.

'Initially because of *Penruth*. He was astounded that we'd been working together and from talking about your acting talent he slid easily into his feelings for you as a person. It was then that I found that what I'd taken to be an illicit meeting arranged between you both, was, in fact, an impulsive one on his side to ease his conscience.' Felix sat up and ran a hand through his hair before shaking his head in barely concealed exasperation. 'Why didn't you explain the situation to me, Frances ...?'

'I doubt you would have believed me, the rage you were in,' she broke in swiftly. 'And why should I have done so? If you thought I was the sort of person to have an affair with a married man then I didn't care what you thought!'

Liar, of course you cared, she told herself scornfully.

'You became rather angry for someone who didn't care,' he replied thoughtfully.

'Oh well, I suppose I did, in a way,' she said crossly. 'I thought we'd become friends over the weeks of working together. I respected your professional opinion of me ...' She stopped. This was dangerous. 'No one likes to be called names,' she added shortly.

There was silence between them for a moment and then Felix said:

'Yes, I can understand that. Can *you* understand that knowing you were the girl involved with Mark at Chichester, and seeing him visit you secretly at your flat, it was quite credible for me to jump to the wrong conclusions?' He held her gaze and she eventually dropped her eyes to her hands, clenched in her lap.

'I suppose it was,' she admitted, and he sat back, satisfied.

'Thank you for allowing me to have my say, Frances. I selfishly hope that you're going to accept my apology.' He lightened his voice deliberately. 'We Scorpions don't like being proved wrong, it doesn't sit well with our personality. I'll even grovel on the floor if you really want me to,' he added persuasively.

Many a night had Frances lain in bed imagining Felix doing just that, with herself standing haughtily over him, but now, somehow, the idea didn't appeal and she said wearily:

'Oh, of course I'll accept your apology, Felix. It all seems so unimportant now and not worth bothering about.'

His eyes narrowed and he replied deliberately: 'Aren't you glad that our misunderstanding has been cleared up?'

She shrugged. 'I suppose so.'

He nodded slowly. 'Rather stupid of me to expect that it should mean as much to you as to myself.' He rose to his feet. 'I hope you won't take your disappointment in me to extend to my mother. She is genuinely fond of you, Frances, and if you can spare the time to look in on her now and again ...' He left the sentence unfinished and Frances stood up without replying.

They began to walk towards the lounge exit.

'Did you watch *Penruth* while you were in Leeds?' Felix asked, and Frances turned in surprise.

'How did you know where I was?'

'Through Gareth, who had it from Zoe,' he explained, holding open the door and following her through.

'Oh, I see. Yes, I did,' she replied absently, realising that the escape to Leeds was no escape at all. 'Were you pleased with the favourable response from the critics?' she asked, making an effort for normality as they collected her coat.

'I'm never fully satisfied with anything I do and can always wish I'd done something differently, but I was able to watch it without squirming too much.' He paused. 'I understand Julian has had quite a number of offers of work resulting from it.'

'Has he? That's good. What is he doing now, do you know?' There was silence and she turned to him, thinking Felix hadn't heard, ready to ask the question again, but was forestalled by him saying slowly:

'He's at the National. I assumed you would have known that.'

Frances stared. 'No. Why should I?'

'I thought you were on close terms with Raynor,' Felix said mildly, and Frances found it necessary to say evenly:

'Julian is a good friend, but a Christmas card is all the correspondence we share.'

'I see. And what about you, Frances?'

'Oh, *Penruth* has more than paid off so far as my career is concerned, so like Mark, you can scrub me off your conscience.' They were, by now, on the steps of the hotel and pulling her coat together Frances said coolly: 'Goodbye, Felix. I suppose this meeting between us had to be made, at some time or another.'

'Can I get you a taxi? It looks as though it's going to rain.'

'No, thank you, I'd rather walk.' She held out her hand with finality and he took it, searching her face with a deeply penetrating look before nodding slightly, and saying formally:

'Goodbye, Frances ... and good luck.'

She ran down the steps and began to walk swiftly home.

There was a message on the pad from Zoe when she reached the flat. It read: 'Agency rang. Someone needs a Rosalind. Ring back and confirm availability—urgent. Looks like this is goodbye again! Zoe.'

Frances rang the agency, confirmed that she had played in *As You Like It* before, that she was available to leave at once, and in less than two hours was on the train for Nottingham.

Frances was with the Playhouse for three months and the pretty violet-blue flowers of the clematis were in full bloom around the front door of Lady Ravenscar's house when she finally decided to pay her a visit.

Simkin admitted her, showing her into the long, gracious room, and then surprised her by saying:

'Lady Ravenscar is not at home at present, Miss Heron. She is with Miss Jessica in Edinburgh.'

'Oh! I'm sorry, I didn't realise ... yes, of course, she must be so pleased about the arrival of her new grandson. Well, perhaps you could tell her I called and ...'

'Do you wish to see Mr Felix?' Simkin asked deferentially, and Frances' mind went blank, quite unable to produce an excuse that would sound convincing on the spur of the moment.

'Is he here? Oh, well ... perhaps he's busy? I mean, I don't ...' She trailed off beneath Simkin's patient look and added feebly : 'If it's convenient, Simkin.'

He inclined his head and left the room quietly.

There wasn't much time for her to collect her scattered wits. Almost immediately the door opened and her panic changed to surprise.

'Why, Gareth! You here as well? How are you?'

Gareth took her hands and held them for a moment, smiling, before replying : 'I'm fine, Frances, and there's no need for me to ask how you are, I can see for myself that you're looking very well! Zoe told me you were working hard at the Playhouse. How did it go?'

'Not too badly, considering my initiation was only one rehearsal with a full cast before going on—live dangerously, that's me!' she replied, laughing as she remembered stepping into the shoes of an actress who had fallen ill on the eve of curtain-up. 'But the plays that followed were not so nerve-racking.' She eyed him with renewed interest. 'You've seen Zoe recently?'

'Yes, indeed. We enjoyed a very good meal together last night, as a matter of fact,' Gareth answered blandly, his dark eyes gleaming with amusement. 'Simkin says you want to see Felix?'

'No!' exclaimed Frances, rather too quickly. 'I came to see Lady Ravenscar, but as she's in Edinburgh Simkin suggested I should see Felix, but if he's busy I ...'

'I wouldn't say he was busy,' Gareth broke in, looking at her closely. 'You haven't seen Zoe since you arrived back?' he asked slowly.

'Why, yes, I have briefly. We've not had a chance to

talk much.' She frowned at his expression and asked a puzzled: 'Why?'

'You obviously haven't heard about the accident.'

A cool hand of fear gripped her heart. 'What accident?' she breathed, and time was suspended for his answer.

'The one Felix was involved in,' Gareth explained, and taking a startled look at her face, added abruptly: 'Frances! Good heavens, girl, come and sit down!'

Frances felt as if her legs had turned to jelly and was aware of the knowledge that she must not faint. Her heart was pounding and her throat swelled and tightened. She was thankful for Gareth's support to the chair and the next thing was to find a glass in her hand and his voice coming from far away, ordering her to drink it slowly.

She did so blindly, his voice becoming stronger. 'Look, Frances, there's no need to panic. It's all over and done with now—at least, the worrying part,' and when Frances dared venture a look at his face she found herself blushing beneath the kindly concern shown there.

'I'm sorry, Gareth. I suppose I ...' She stopped. Excuses were going to be pointless after that little give away. 'What has happened to him?'

Gareth seated himself opposite. 'Well now, let me see ... Felix was driving home late one evening, about a couple of months ago, when he became involved in a police chase. It seems that four youths had broken into a warehouse and had to make a quick getaway, and unfortunately Felix crossed their path. He didn't stand a chance. After hitting the Lancia they crashed into a shop front. Two of them were killed outright.'

'How dreadful,' Frances said, beginning to shake again. 'And Felix?'

Gareth leaned forward and removed the glass from her hands, pretending not to notice the state she was in.

'Felix has been extremely lucky, coming out of it with numerous superficial cuts and bruises, one very deep cut on his forehead and a cracked rib.' He rubbed the side of his nose pensively. 'What did cause us some concern was a splinter of glass that lodged itself in his right eye. He had an emergency operation immediately on arrival at the hospital and it was touch and go whether the eye could be saved. We know now that it has been.' Gareth handed her back the glass and watched her take a sip. 'Margaret has borne up under the strain remarkably well, she's an amazingly resilient old lady, and now that Felix is convalescing and the danger is over I was able to persuade her to go and stay with Jessica for a while.' He stood up and strolled over to the window. 'Will you see him, Frances?'

'I don't think I ... He won't want to be bothered ...'

Gareth turned quickly, his dark eyes shrewdly appraising her.

'He knows someone's here,' he said quietly. 'He'll ask who it was.'

Frances rested her head in her hands, completely unprepared by the force of her emotions and unable to hide them from Gareth. What a fool she was! Only a fool would have kidded herself that Felix meant nothing to her. It didn't matter that all he felt for her was a physical attraction, her feelings may have started off that way, but a deeper feeling had crept up on her, one which she had refused to acknowledge. What a way to find out the truth! The mere thought of Felix hurt was painful and she clung to Gareth's assurance that the danger was over. He wouldn't say that unless ... Her stomach lurched and she sat up quickly, asking urgently:

'He *is* all right, Gareth? You're not just saying that ...'

'In time he'll be almost as good as new. The head wound will leave a scar, but his sight will be unimpaired.'

Gareth gave an exclamation of concern and crossed to her, and she rose to meet him. Putting his hands on her shoulders he said compassionately: 'Had I the slightest inkling how you felt I would have told you differently, but I had no idea ...'

She gave a wobbly smile. 'Neither had I. I'm sorry to be such a fool,' and she fumbled in her pocket for a handkerchief and blew her nose. 'I wonder why Zoe didn't write and let me know?'

Gareth frowned in thought. 'I didn't see her myself during the critical week and then I may have mentioned it casually, in passing. We doctors like to leave our work behind us, you know, and if Zoe was not aware of the situation either she probably forgot to mention it.' He paused. 'Will you see him, Frances? I'm sure he'd be pleased if you did.'

Frances shook her head uncertainly. 'We've met once in nine months, Gareth, and then our relationship was strained.'

'Nevertheless, the visit from a pretty girl is bound to cheer him up. It gets rather lonely, you know, not being able to see ...' Gareth allowed the words to linger provocatively between them and watched the indecision change as she replied weakly:

'Very well, I'll see him if you think ...'

'Good!' Gareth broke in quickly before she had second thoughts. 'He's still bandaged, so you needn't worry about how you look—tear-stained, I mean.' He was taking her across the room as he spoke. 'But you'll find that blind people, however temporary, become supersensitive, and voices can be a giveaway.'

She stopped, halting their progress. 'Gareth, you won't say anything to Felix, will you?' she began awkwardly. 'About me, I mean. It's all on my side, you see, and I couldn't bear for him to know how I feel.'

He shook his head reproachfully and opened the door.

Ahead of them, through the library, was the conservatory. 'Felix is out there today, feeling bored, so beware. I'll leave you to him, I was just on my way out when you arrived.' He squeezed her arm. 'Good luck, Frances. 'Bye for now,' and before she could protest she was gently pushed towards the conservatory door and found herself alone with Felix.

'Who was it, Gareth?' Felix asked lazily. He was lying in a reclining lounger, dressed in slacks and sweater, the door to the garden being partially open, letting in the May sunshine. A table by his side held a bowl of fruit and a portable radio, and the daily paper was spread out on the other chair, as if Gareth had been reading from it.

'Gareth?' Felix said sharply, sitting up during the silence caused by her stunned appraisal of the scene.

Frances was galvanised into speech and action, walking hesitantly over and saying: 'It's all right, Felix, it's only me. Gareth has left.'

Felix turned his head in the direction of her voice, body movement suspended, and then he visibly relaxed and answered in a drawling voice:

'Well, well, so it's only "me", is it? Hullo, Frances, how kind of you to visit.'

'Hullo, Felix,' Frances replied. Don't think about loving him. She must be rational. Don't think about the way she wanted to rush over and cling to him, to feel his body against hers, to have his hands warm and possessively holding her, his lips seeking her own. Her eyes devoured the lower half of his face, the brown skin curiously opaque, the mouth stretched into a half-smile, as if unsure of himself.

It was this unsureness, this vulnerability, that was nearly her undoing.

'No, please, don't get up,' she said hastily, as he began to move. 'How are you, Felix?'

'As well as can be expected, thank you,' he answered politely, making her desperately sure that she should not have come.

'I ... I had no idea ... none at all, that you'd been in an accident.'

'Really?'

He didn't believe her. 'I came to see Lady Ravenscar and Gareth told me,' she explained helplessly.

'Mother's loss is my gain, it seems.' Felix paused. 'So you didn't know,' he added matter-of-factly.

'Not a thing. I shall have something to say to Zoe, not writing!'

He smiled rather wryly. 'I don't believe your friend altogether approves of me. Come here, Frances. I can't bear disembodied voices,' he ordered, stretching out a hand. Frances hesitated momentarily and then stepped forward, placing her own in his grasp. He lifted it to his face, very close to his lips. 'Mmm, you smell nice ... what is it?'

Frances could feel her pulse jumping away like mad against his palm. 'Nothing outstanding. Honeysuckle, I think ... I can't remember,' she answered incoherently.

'Whatever it is, it suits you. I'm glad you've come, Frances. It shows you've forgiven me for past hurts and I shall take full advantage of the situation and bask in your pity.'

'Rubbish!' said Frances, laughing. 'If you truly needed pitying you'd hate it.'

'How well you know me, dear girl,' he replied lightly. 'The truth is, I'm bored. I feel like quarrelling with someone, and we do it so well, don't we? Pull up a chair,' and when she made no move, he added: 'Can you stay?'

Her voice became teasing, basking in the knowledge that he wanted her company. 'Yes, of course I can, but I need my hand before I can fetch the chair.'

He smiled. 'So you do.' She was released and he waited
while she pulled forward the other chair. 'What colour
are you wearing, Frances? It's rather dark behind these
damned bandages and I want to imagine what you look
like.'

A rush of emotion swept over her and controlling a
tell-tale quiver, she answered flippantly: 'Miss Heron is
wearing a lightweight wool suit in a delightful shade of
heather mixture, with cream accessories. She is also
wearing a short haircut, acquired at Maison Elaine of
Nottingham ...'

'Good heavens!' broke in Felix, sitting up. 'Are you,
indeed? That takes a bit of imagining. Let me feel it.'

Warily, Frances leaned forward and allowed his fingers to run through the short hair. 'For Rosalind, when
she pretends to be a boy,' she explained, closing her eyes
with pleasure and curbing the desire to cling to his
hands, holding them to her face. 'And it will curl so,' she
added weakly, as he withdrew.

'Hmm ... I shall have to wait judgment on that until
I can see for myself, but it feels nice, and the rest of you
sounds delightful. Thank you, I can see you quite plainly
now.' Felix leaned back comfortably. 'Tell me what
you've been doing, Frances.'

Afterwards Frances was astounded at how quickly the
time flew by. When she finally left she walked the park,
not seeing anything or anyone, only remembering Felix
as he had looked when she said goodbye, hearing his
voice, dry and slightly mocking ...

Coming finally to terms with the fact that she loved
him.

CHAPTER EIGHT

FRANCES was lucky enough to get a job with a television commercial company, which enabled her to stay on in London, at least for a while. She called in to see Felix every day, to read the paper out loud to him, or sometimes to just sit and talk. What she was doing was short-sighted and emotionally dangerous, but she didn't care. She was taking day by day as it came and thanking fate for whatever crumb it could offer.

And then, right out of the blue, fate offered a good job. A new Tom Stoppard play to be put on in the West End ... and a fantastic chance for her. A few weeks ago she would have been over the moon at the offer, but now all ambitions had paled. She auditioned because she knew that life would have to continue once Felix had no further need of her company, and was told that 'they'd let her know'.

The day after this audition Frances walked into the conservatory to find it empty and putting down papers and books on the table she stepped out into the garden. She saw Felix sitting on a seat, his back to her, and her heart sank. Her time of usefulness was over. She crossed the grass, calling out with assumed cheerfulness:

'Hullo, Felix! I see they've taken off the bandages.' She stopped, the words abruptly cut as he turned, and she found herself staring at him in dismay. Emotion choked in her throat. Gareth should have warned her he'd look like this, she thought angrily, drawing a deep breath and trying to conceal her initial shock.

'What's it like being able to see at last? I expect it's rather strange,' she managed.

'Hullo, Frances. Yes, they unbound me this morning and I'm to sit in the sun on doctor's orders.' Felix watched her move round the seat to sit next to him. 'Poor girl. Didn't Gareth tell you what a mess I am?' He smiled sardonically. 'Never mind, I won't blame you if you don't look too often.'

'Don't be ridiculous,' she replied calmly, every nerve in her body geared to casualness. 'If you're asking for my sympathy you'll be unlucky.' She looked critically at his face. He was wearing dark glasses, but they did not hide the ugly wound that ran from the middle of his forehead, high up near the hair-line, to finish a couple of inches to the side of the right eye. 'Not a pretty sight, I agree, but it'll fade in time, surely,' she announced at last, tilting her head consideringly. 'In fact, Felix, I think it will enhance your looks, rather than mar them.'

'Indeed?' His brows rose and the scar distorted.

'Yes. There's a demonic look about you now—the ladies will come flocking!'

He gave a bark of cynical laughter. 'Heaven forbid!' adding dryly: 'What a clever girl you are, Frances. Very diplomatic.'

'I don't know what you mean,' she replied smoothly.

'Liar!' He frowned. 'Where did you get to yesterday?'

Frances felt a silly stab of pleasure that he'd missed her. 'I went after a job—I do have to earn a living, you know.' She gestured to the dark glasses. 'Does this mean that you're allowed to read for yourself now?'

'No, it does not ... you can't get out of your duties like that.'

'Then I'll go and fetch ...'

He caught her hand as she rose to go. 'Stay and talk,' he demanded, pulling her gently down again, retaining her hand and increasing the pressure slightly when she tried to free herself.

With colour in her cheeks, Frances asked lightly: 'What shall we talk about?'

He smiled lazily. 'About how much better it is, seeing

you instead of imagining you.'

She caught her breath. This was much more like the Felix of old, and infinitely more dangerous. 'Have they washed their hands of you now?' she asked hurriedly.

'Unfortunately not ... I believe there are some more tests to be done before I can fly away to the sun.'

Her eyes moved quickly to his face. 'You're going away?'

He nodded, a mocking smile hovering. 'Will you miss me, Frances?'

'Why, yes, of course I will.' His thumb was gently caressing her palm, making her flesh tingle.

'Do you know, I rather think I shall miss you too!' When there was no response to this, he continued: 'On the advice of my good doctor friend, I'm to go away, to rest and relax in the sun.' He gave an exasperated sigh. 'As though I haven't been doing enough resting lately!'

'Where shall you go?' asked Frances, desolation spreading over her.

He shrugged. 'The idea was only sprung on me this morning. I haven't had time to consider.' He paused. 'Have you anywhere you can suggest?'

Frances looked round the old-fashioned walled garden thoughtfully. It was very quiet. The roses and the border flowers made a bright splash of colour among the cool greenery of the shrubs and trees.

'I've been told that Corfu is a lovely island,' she heard herself saying calmly.

In the ensuing silence she watched a sparrow tentatively fly down to the sundial in the centre of the small lawn, quickly take up a morsel of breadcrumb and fly off again.

'Corfu?' Felix turned to stare at her. 'Yes, it is ... but I'd only go to Corfu if you came with me.' His tone was matter-of-fact as he watched her face.

'Then Corfu it is,' Frances replied, looking at him fully

for the first time since burning her boats. She wished she could see his eyes behind the dark glasses. She could perhaps have learned something from them. The frown was very visible. 'You've sold me on the idea,' she added, giving a decisive nod.

'The devil I have!' He broke away from her and leaned forward, staring down at the ground. 'You'd be getting a bad bargain—do you realise that?' The words sounded curiously angry.

'I know the rules, Felix.'

'I'm not so sure that I do.' He looked at her sharply. 'Why have you changed your mind, Frances?'

'Isn't that the lady's prerogative?' she asked flippantly. 'Is it necessary for the third degree, Felix?'

'Yes, I think it is. You were very articulate on the reasons for your refusal before.'

'That was over a year ago. Perhaps I've decided to kill off my guilt complexes!' She hoped for a smile, but the austere expression didn't waver. She felt a sudden chill. 'Have I left it too late, perhaps? There's someone else?'

'No. There's no one I'd rather take with me,' he answered shortly.

Relief spread over her. 'So what's the problem, Felix?' and she gave a tentative smile.

'I want you to be absolutely certain that you know why you're coming. I don't want us to be half-way across Europe and you change your mind.'

'How ridiculous you are! You don't expect me to behave like that, surely?' she burst out, half exasperated and half amused.

'No, I don't.'

'Then what's the fuss about, for goodness' sake! Look, Felix, it's not every day that I ...' Her voice petered out and she bit her lip. This line of argument was best shelved. It was, in fact, her weakest. She was not particularly proud of her inexperience in such matters and had no intention of letting Felix know. Handing over one's virtue as late as twenty-six could have certain hang-ups—such as the idea of living happily ever after, and he wouldn't chance the possible traumas just for a few weeks in the sun with her. She would deal with any personal traumas if and when they came.

Frances put a hand to her brow and gave a helpless laugh. 'Felix! We're even fighting over this!' she protested.

He shook his head. 'We're merely getting things into perspective. You know why I want you to come with me. It seems only fair that I should know your reasons. No matter what you may think, I don't embark on such a relationship lightly, and I'm sure neither do you.'

'No, well ...' Her brain was working furiously. This wasn't going the way she had planned it at all! She ought to have known that Felix, for all his charm and easy talk, wouldn't accept her change of mind unquestioningly. She decided to keep to as near the truth as possible and took a deep breath. 'All right, Felix ... my reason is this,' and she carefully placed her hand against the side of his cheek. He gave an imperceptible flinch and then caught it with his own, keeping it there. Her palm felt on fire.

'You see?' she asked softly. 'Even after a year it's still the same ... so my reasons are the same as yours. I've mistrusted this physical attraction, but now I realise that running away from it is running away from living, and life's too short. So I'll come away with you, Felix, and we'll give the fireworks a chance to burn themselves out,' and Frances didn't add that for her she doubted that they ever would. She withdrew her hand and clasped both together on her lap.

Felix was leaning back, legs outstretched, the implacable look gone, to be replaced by one of deep contemplation. There was a long silence before he drawled: 'I'll

accept your reasons, Frances,' and sitting up, reflected:
'We'll have to do something about your passport. What
about this job that's in the offing?'

'Oh, I didn't get it,' she said, and smiled ruefully.
'That's the way it goes sometimes,' and Felix nodded,
and again she wished he wasn't hiding behind the dark
glasses.

'So you aren't contracted to anything at the moment?'
he asked, and she shook her head. Nothing, apart from
you, Felix, she told him silently.

'Is there anyone who's likely to be against this deci-
sion of yours?' Again she shook her head. There was,
but she could deal with Zoe.

'No, I'm completely alone in the world and answerable to no one,' she replied calmly.

His hand came up to lightly touch a curl lying deli-
cately against the curve of her cheek.

'I'll not let you regret it, Frances,' he said gently, and
then leaned forward and brushed his mouth against hers,
a wisp of a kiss, lingering briefly, promising. 'There,
we've sealed our bargain.' He stood up, saying briskly:
'I'm moving back to my flat tomorrow. I have some loose
ends to tie up at the studios, and the police want to see
me regarding statements for the accident. I'll telephone
you as soon as I know the exact date. We'll fly, of
course.'

'I'll be ready,' she promised, her head in a whirl, not
daring to look at him fully in case he should read more
in her eyes than she wanted him to know.

'And you're quite sure, Frances, that you want to go
ahead with this?' he asked steadily, and she replied:

'Quite sure.'

Lying in the shade of a protruding rock, a discarded
book by her side, Frances remembered those words and
wished she could still feel so confident.

In front of her was a calm, glittering sea, lapping the curve of the white, dazzling beach. Behind her, sheltering the small, deserted bay, towered thickly wooded hills of pine, cedar and cypress, which swept right down to the coast, finishing in hard rock cliffs. Hugged tightly to these cliffs was the small inn of Astrakeri.

Astrakeri! How beautiful were the sounds of the Greek names, as beautiful as the island itself. Frances remembered her first sight of it as the BA plane approached the cluster of islands dotted far below in the bluest of blue seas; seven islands, looking as though they had been dropped from a painter's palette. Corfu was easily recognisable, being the most northerly, distinctive because of its long sickle shape, lush with fertile valleys, hills of dense olive trees, and Mount Pantocrator, bare and rocky, rising steeply from the sea, north of the airport.

Frances gave a sigh and rose, collecting together her things. The sun blazed down on her skin and the sand struck with almost unbearable heat to the soles of her feet and she quickly slipped on her sandals. She was glad to leave the beach and savour the refreshing cool of the steep path that zig-zagged its way up between tall, dark trees. Perfume was everywhere, a mixture of orange-blossom and pine, olive and cypress, and coming out of the gloomy shadows, her feet treading softly on the fallen pine needles, she made her usual stop to catch her breath.

She was in a clearing, an almost fairy-like glade, and the riot of colour always came as a joyous shock every time she came to it. The profusion of flowers was like a jungle. Roses had been allowed to grow to unusual heights, fine walls of wisteria hung like tapestry and honeysuckle reached out to tempt with its heady perfume. An idyllic setting ... for what should have been an idyllic holiday!

Frances sank down by a bank of arum lilies growing out of the moist, shady undergrowth, and hugged her knees, going over the last few days in her mind—an occupation she had indulged in more often than was good for her morale.

They had started off on the wrong foot, she thought miserably, with Felix withdrawn and almost formal, and herself racked first with a stupid shyness and then, because of his reserve, with equally stupid nervousness. By the time they had landed at Corfu airport Felix was beginning to sound like a travel brochure and she was sure it was with relief on both sides that a third person joined them as they passed through customs.

Spiro Stephanides was this welcome addition—a giant of a man, his battered peaked cap doffed by the largest hands Frances had ever seen. He was standing by a dusty black car, and seeing Felix, he stepped forward, shaking his hand enthusiastically, his leathery face creased in a beaming smile, his rapid Greek a profuse and voluble greeting.

Spiro had driven them across the island to Astrakeri, on the north coast, where Josef and Sofia, the owners of the inn where Felix had booked for them to stay, had repeated this welcome, showing great affection towards Felix, who was obviously well known to them.

The inn was small, but charming, having only three guest bedrooms, two of which were allocated to Felix and herself. This was the first slight shock to Frances. Not that she wasn't grateful to Felix in not wishing to offend the proprieties of his friends and cause her any embarrassment, but it wasn't conducive to breaking down this restraint between them. And since then, nothing had happened to offend anyone!

They had spent two outwardly pleasant days, acting like any other holidaymakers, lazing on the beach or swimming in the sea. They had explored the archipelago of small rocks along the shoreline, Felix rowing Josef's boat, and they would peer down through the crystal-clear water. There, underwater plants wove to and fro, fish darted in and out of them, flashing bright colours, spider crabs scuttled among anemones clinging to the rocks on which sea-urchins clustered, spiky and dangerous. And when they became tired of the shore, Spiro drove them inland, where peasant girls laughed and giggled on the backs of donkeys as they made their way to work in the fields, and the goatherd gave his shrill whistle, urging his flock from the road to allow the car to pass freely. There was a rustic simplicity about the island that enchanted Frances and she was soon under its spell.

And at night she went alone to her bed, leaving Felix downstairs talking to Josef and the other Corfiote men who gathered regularly in the inn. She soon realised that Greek women were banished from important affairs, such as *kaló* or *kakó*, good or bad, of the local wine crop, affairs of state or the day's fishing haul. She learned to recognise the best Greek noise caused by *kéfi*, that release of inspired high spirits which often resulted in spontaneous music and dancing. She felt frustrated in more ways than one ... life seemed to be holding so much in store for her, and yet was dangling it tantalisingly just out of reach.

Then, when she had resolved to ask Felix outright what the matter was, someone called Theodore Alexi-akis of Athens managed to put a spoke in her wheel.

They had gone for a walk after their evening meal and on returning to the inn decided to swim, for the air was still warm. As they plunged into the water the phosphorescence turned their bodies into a golden green glow beneath the surface and when they finally emerged, to lie on the sand, fireflies made their nightly sortie from the olive groves, skimming across the water, their lights winking on and off, making a strange fairy-like glow.

Frances, lying flat on her back on the sand, turned her head to look at Felix. The moon was bright enough for her to see that his eyes were closed, and she leaned over to brush the fall of hair from his forehead, saying softly :

'Does it still hurt?'

His eyes opened. 'The wound? No, not at all now.'

'I'm glad. You're looking much better,' she told him, and impulsively planted a light kiss along the jagged line, her wet body briefly touching his. Felix's arms came round her and pulled her to him.

It was their first real kiss since arriving on Corfu and it was packed with all the intensity and passion that the previous days had stored up. Somehow Frances found herself lying once more on the sand, Felix searching her eyes, cheeks, the hollow of her throat with tiny kisses.

A wave of happiness swept over her and she returned his kisses with mounting fervour, so relieved that he still wanted her. When he at last lifted himself away, hands either side, she smiled up at him.

'You taste of salt,' she murmured, running her fingers through his thick hair, trailing them along the breadth of his shoulders.

'You look and taste good enough to eat,' Felix said, rolling over and standing up in a single continuous movement. He bent to pick up her beach robe and threw it round her, effortlessly pulling her to her feet.

With his arms round her shoulders and her own round his waist Frances drew a contented breath as they walked back across the sand towards the inn.

A pair of headlights came sweeping round the curve of the road as they emerged from the cliff path, halting outside the inn.

'I wonder what Spiro wants?' Frances murmured, as the huge, dark figure loomed towards them.

'He's come to take me into the airport. I'm flying to

Athens in a couple of hours,' Felix replied, voice expressionless.

Frances stopped short and turned an incredulous face towards him.

'You're what?' she asked.

'I'm flying to Athens,' he repeated, calling out something in Greek to Spiro who waved a hand and turned back into the inn. 'I have some business to attend to, you've heard me mention my good friend, Theo Alexiakis ... I can't get out of it, I'm afraid,' he explained, and before Frances could utter another word, he pulled her to him, gave her a quick, hard kiss and pushed her into the inn, telling her laconically : 'It'll take a day.'

And here she was, living off memories of that brief interlude on the beach, still on her own ... and wishing that Theodore Alexiakis would keep his business troubles to himself! Spiro had looked after her with dog-like devotion, and Josef and Sofia communicated as best they could, obviously sympathetic towards the *thespoînis* in her abandoned state ... which had stretched now into two days.

A call made her look up to see Sofia standing in the porchway of the inn, holding a carafe and a glass. Frances made her way over, accepting the ice cold, fresh lemon drink gratefully.

'You like, *Thespoînis* Frances?' Sofia asked shyly.

Frances smiled her thanks. 'It's lovely, Sofia,' and after taking a sip, she asked hopefully : '*Kyrios* Felix has not yet returned?'

Sofia shook her head. 'Not yet, *thespoînis*, but he will come,' she promised, something in her eyes causing Frances a brief confusion, and yet instinctively bringing them to a closer understanding of each other.

Thanking her again, Frances returned the empty glass and after saying that the evening meal would be in half an hour, Sofia re-entered the inn.

Frances ate by herself at the small round table in the garden, a lighted candle adding to the romantic setting. Not even the delicious brochettes of beef which Sofia had cooked in an aromatic herbal sauce, or the wine that Josef freely poured, could dispel the ridiculousness of the situation. She put on a cheerful face for them but couldn't disguise the fact that she was all the time waiting for the sound of Spiro's car sweeping round the curve of the road.

It must have done so the following morning while she was having her early morning swim in the sea. As she panted slightly, out of breath from the steep wooded climb, Frances suddenly saw the familiar black car parked outside the inn. Breathless now for another reason, she ran lightly up the stairs to find Felix's door open and him standing by the window. As this looked out across the bay he must have seen her approach and hearing her footfalls on the landing, turned and walked across the room.

'Good morning, *Thespoînis* Heron,' he said, lazily, his eyes taking in her gleaming, golden body and glowing face in a satisfactory sweep.

Frances felt the old rush of excitement go through her at his look.

'Good morning, *Kyrie* Ravenscar,' she responded, a tremble in her voice which she covered hastily by asking if he had breakfasted yet.

'No. I was waiting for you,' Felix replied. 'Sofia has everything prepared at our table in the garden.' He looked at her hair, clinging damply to her head, and throwing over a towel added: 'Do you have to change? I'm famished.'

Frances shook her head and began to rub her hair briskly. 'No, I'm almost dry anyway, and my wrap is quite respectable, isn't it?' she asked, throwing down the towel and tying the cord of her bathing robe.

Following her back down the stairs, her long legs giving him the utmost pleasure, Felix replied dryly : 'Adequate would be a better word, I think,' and Frances flashed him a knowing grin over her shoulder.

The delicious grilled fish that Sofia brought out to them was served with a rapid stream of Greek, which was interspersed with the occasional glance at Frances.

When she had disappeared for the coffee, Frances asked curiously :

'What was that all about, Felix?'

He began to spread honey on to a roll as he spoke. 'Today is one of the many feast days and as such is a holiday. Something to do with Saint Spiridon, Corfu's patron saint, and the island celebrates the occasion with processions and music, food and wine.'

'I'm all for celebrating an occasion,' said Frances, slanting a glance at him as she dug her teeth into a melon. '*Mētrio*, Sofia,' she added quickly, as Sofia brought out the tray of coffee and handed a slightly sweetened one to her.

'*Skéto*, Sofia,' responded Felix, his amused eyes upon Frances as Sofia passed him his cup of black Turkish coffee, but before he could comment on her provocative observation, Spiro arrived unexpectedly, loath to interrupt, but feeling it necessary to do so.

Hat in hand, Spiro smiled apologetically to Frances and then launched into rapid speech, arms gesticulating wildly, to Felix. When he had finished he gave Frances his usual dignified half-bow and backed out of the garden, the sound of the car accelerating away coming almost immediately.

'And what was *that* all about?' Frances asked, highly delighted by Spiro's performance.

Felix hesitated, pouring a drink of fresh orange for them both before answering casually : 'I have a small villa near here which has been having some alterations.

The plumbers have at last finished, and as Spiro has been breathing heavily down their necks for the past three weeks, he's overjoyed to be able to tell me that we can move in tomorrow.' He raised his glass to his lips, his gaze steadily upon her while he drank.

To her disgust Frances found a blush sweeping over her and quickly lowered her lashes, unable to meet his look. 'I didn't know you had your own house,' she murmured. 'How long have you owned it?'

Felix pursed his lips in reflection. 'About five years.' He rose to his feet and Frances followed suit. 'Sofia's sister, Maria, comes in every day to cook and clean. It's an ideal holiday retreat.'

'Is it far from Astrakeri?' she asked, preceding him into the inn.

'No, no, less than a kilometre along the coast,' he replied, adding quickly: 'What's the matter? Have you hurt your foot, Frances? You seem to be limping.'

Admitting to the pain under her heel, Frances squinted down at it, wondering what was causing the stinging jabs every time she put on pressure, and announced, 'I think I have a splinter.'

'We'll have a look at it,' proposed Felix, walking into his room in search of the first aid box. 'It doesn't do to ignore anything like that, however trivial.'

Frances followed him in and sat down, offering her foot to him for inspection.

'Hmm ... a splinter from a pine needle ... yes, here it comes,' Felix said softly, easing it out competently with a pair of tweezers and then dabbing with cotton wool and antiseptic. He pressed a plaster into place and looked up enquiringly. 'Better?'

Frances stood up and tested her weight. 'Yes, thank you, much better,' and as Felix rose from his crouching position to stand facing her she raised her eyes to his face and taking her courage in both hands, whispered: 'I've missed you.'

She found that, after all, she could not wait to see his reaction, her eyes falling away from his face. The situation suddenly appalled her. What would she do if he had changed his mind? Or if he hadn't and then soon tired of her? A desolate thought! Her eyes flew back in a moment of swift panic.

Felix was viewing her with a serious, thoughtful expression on his face. His hands came up and grasped her arms, drawing her to him, and she clutched at his shirt, feeling the erratic thumping of his heart against her hand.

She made no move to stop his caresses and the robe slipped unheeded from her shoulders to the floor. I love you, Felix, she cried out silently, as his mouth parted hers, leaving her limp with longing, and it was some seconds before she was aware of the persistent knocking at the door accompanied by a volley of Greek words. Felix lifted his head attentively and called a brief answer and the footsteps receded.

Frances closed her eyes in resignation, not knowing whether to burst into hysterical laughter or tears.

'What did Sofia want?' she murmured into his chest.

Felix brushed his lips along her smooth, rounded shoulder and said calmly: 'She says that the bus that's taking us to Corfu for the festivities will be coming down the lane in fifteen minutes.' He rescued the wrap from the floor and draped it round her, holding it in both hands, keeping her a prisoner. 'I said we would be on it.'

'Naturally,' she agreed gravely, maintaining her dignity, and refusing to see the smile in his eyes. 'We must pay our respects to Saint Spiridon. You have nothing else on the agenda, have you?' she asked innocently, eyes wide and enquiring.

'Nothing that can't be put off for a better time and

place,' he replied smoothly, adding: 'Oh, and Sofia also says that there's a peasant dress on your bed which should fit you. She'll be honoured if you'll wear it. Everyone will be in feast-day costume and it will enhance the *thespoînis's* beauty. Sofia's words, but ones that I endorse.' He turned her round and propelled her gently in to her own room.

'Oh, how lovely!' she breathed, gazing at the green shot silk dress with its pretty embroidered muslin apron. She lifted a glowing face. 'Does she really mean me to wear this? It looks new!'

'Yes, of course she does—it probably belonged to one of her daughters.' His eyes glittered. 'If you have any difficulties with the hooks, just shout, 'and he was half-way through the door when he stopped. 'Frances, may I ask you a question?'

She looked up quickly, attuned to something in his voice that caused a flicker of apprehension. 'Yes, of course you may.'

'The truth is, and has been, rather lacking in our relationship, right from our first meeting. I shall be grateful if ... you can bear this in mind.' He was facing her now, one hand raised to the door. 'Why did you give up your part in the Tom Stoppard play?'

There was an almost hypnotic intensity that held her eyes to his.

She swallowed. 'H—how did you know I did?'

'Because it was at my instigation that you were offered the part.'

'I see.' It became, after all, easy to speak the truth. 'I gave it up because if there was a choice between the Stoppard and being with you, then I'd sooner be with you.'

A rapid exclamation was directed up the stairs, piercing the growing awareness between them. Felix smiled his slow, lazy smile.

'Another time, another place,' he promised, and then was gone.

Twenty minutes later Frances found herself being jogged and rattled up and down, side to side, in the most amazing bus she had ever seen. The windows were empty of glass and the single deck was packed with bodies—and not only human ones, animals too, plus crates of fruit and vegetables.

There was an air of holiday spirit about the passengers, all dressed in their best, with much laughing and shouting, accompanied by the tooting of the bus horn every time the driver rounded a bend, which was, by nature of their journey through the mountain ridge, often. Frances had long ceased to worry about their safety, no one else seemed to be concerned. She sat between Sofia and Sofia's younger sister Maria, who had inherited the family habit of smiling and nodding happily whenever Frances caught her eye.

The two sisters carried on a continual conversation across her, and as Frances heard the word *anglítha* repeated more than once, knew it was mostly about herself and Felix, and it was probably as well that she couldn't understand it. The rest of the passengers could, however, much to her embarrassment, and the safest person to look at was Felix, which was no hardship.

He was sitting opposite her, next to Josef. A basket of doves was in the aisle separating them, giving a musical addition to the chatter and laughter. As the olive groves rushed by at an alarming speed Frances suddenly realised that he was smiling at her and she found herself smiling unreservedly back. She felt the sweet stirrings of pleasure rise up within her, grateful for any small crumb that came her way and glad that he knew she loved him. Pretence for her was gone. Restraint was gone. She was happy.

He looked very handsome, she thought, her eyes devouring him, an ache growing in her throat. With an open white shirt, crisp and fresh by Sofia's careful laundering, and a gay neckerchief provided by Josef, Felix had a feast-day look about him too, his scarred face giving him a rakish air. She herself was virtually unrecognisable as the Frances she knew—lace, ribbons and costume all adding to the unreality of the day.

It was a few moments before she realised that Felix had spoken to her and she smiled, giving a quick shake of the head and raising her brows in question. He understood that she had not heard him and leaned forward across the doves, saying:

'Frances, will you marry me?'

There was no doubt that she had heard correctly. Next to her Sofia began to chuckle, and as quick translations were passed down the bus, they became the centre of attention again, heads turning to look, smiles broad.

Felix was waiting patiently. 'And I love you very much,' he added as an afterthought, the tawny eyes belying his outward composure.

Frances caught her breath. Only Felix Ravenscar would bring a girl away on an illicit holiday and propose marriage on a crowded bus! Love and laughter exploded inside her, her eyes brimming over at his impudence.

She was being encouraged to answer. Sofia and Maria were nudging her, nodding at Felix with approval ... the whole bus, including the driver, was waiting in fevered anticipation for her answer, although they all knew what it was going to be.

'Well?' he asked, taking her hands across the aisle.

'Thank you, Felix, I should like to marry you,' she replied, 'and I love you too.'

Her reply was again translated and a cheer went up. The bus swerved round a corner and pulled to a violent halt, everyone falling, crates and animals rocking. The passengers filed out with what, Frances now realised, was the usual Corfiote volubility, and feeling suddenly, ridiculously shy, she allowed Felix to lift her down the steps and swing her to the ground.

The first person she saw was Spiro, grinning broadly, dressed in an amazingly dapper suit, and looking odd without his shabby peaked cap. Then she saw Zoe ... and Gareth! and Zoe was dressed in an almost identical dress to her own!

In a flash the two girls were in each other's arms, spluttering greetings, and Gareth was clasping Felix by the hand while Spiro was saying:

'I bring them from the airport in damn good time, eh, *Kyrie* Felix?'

'Zoe, Gareth, I can't believe it ...!' Frances began, and then Felix was taking her to one side, saying quietly: 'Frances, this is my very good friend, Theodore Alexiakis,' and she found her hand taken and firmly grasped by a dark, good-looking Greek, who smiled, and said earnestly:

'I am overjoyed to meet the bride-to-be of Felix. I have waited for a long time for this to happen. Now that I look—I understand. Frances, I wish you have every happiness,' and he raised her hand to his lips.

Suddenly everything fell into place ... the two rooms at Astrakeri, the pretty costume, why Zoe and Gareth had been flown out, and why they were now walking down the cool corridors of the British Vice-Consulate.

'The man's mad, completely mad!' she murmured, lifting her face to seek Felix, and holding his gaze through the small group of people between them, basking in his smile. Sofia thrust a posy of flowers into her hands and tweaked a ribbon here, straightened a lace there.

'Sofia, is it really a feast day?' Frances asked, her eyes still upon Felix, who was now talking to two officials.

Sofia laughed and nodded, her headdress and curls bobbing.

'Yes, *thespoînis*, you wait and see. Soon we will make music and dance and there will be much eating and drinking.' She glanced significantly at the disappearing backs of Felix and Gareth. 'Afterwards you will join us.' She gave a sigh of pleasure. 'How beautiful you look, *thespoînis*. *Kyrios* Felix will love you much.'

Theo Alexiakis appeared now, holding out a courteous hand.

'I have the honour to, how do you say, give you away to my friend, Felix. You are quite ready, Frances?' and returning his smile, Frances took his hand and allowed him to lead her to an adjoining room, Zoe falling demurely behind.

Feeling calm and serene, Frances took her place beside Felix, warm happiness spreading over her as their eyes met, eyes full of love and tenderness.

When Frances came out into the sunlight once more she was wearing a plain gold band around her finger and despite the dreamlike state she was in, knew that she was now, quite definitely, Frances Ravenscar.

As Sofia predicted, the feast-day festivities were exhilarating, but soon it was time to take Gareth and Zoe to the airport where they were to catch the plane back to England.

Zoe hugged her hard, face glowing. 'Frances, did you ever dream that your wedding would be like this?' she demanded. 'I can't tell you how thrilled I am that everything has turned out so wonderfully. I can't say any more or I'll bawl my eyes out!' and her choking laugh could easily have been a sob. She managed to add, however: 'Will you wish me luck, too, Frankie?' and rather diffidently held out her hand.

'You're engaged! Oh, Zoe, I am glad!' exclaimed Frances, giving her friend a warm embrace and turning to kiss Gareth as he stood, smiling, by their side. 'Gareth, I'm so happy for you.'

'Thank you, Frances.' He turned to Zoe. 'Come along, darling. Our flight has been called.' Shaking hands with Felix and Theo, Gareth took Zoe firmly by the arm and led her away, both turning to wave before disappearing out of sight.

The return to Astrakeri was in the comparative comfort of Spiro's car. As she sat in Felix's arms, Frances asked:

'How long do these feast days go on?'

Felix settled her more comfortably against his chest and replied: 'I believe this one lasts two days,' and they looked out of the window at the musicians playing for the benefit of the people still dancing in the streets.

'Theo's house was beautiful,' Frances said dreamily. 'All those lights strung from the trees—it was like something out of a film! How kind he is.'

Felix nodded, holding her closer. 'We have Theo to thank for a great deal ... he took over all the legal proceedings completely.'

'And that gorgeous food,' she enthused. 'Delectable sticks of meat and mushrooms—what do they call them, Felix?'

'Souvlaka.'

'Souvlaka,' she repeated obediently. 'Where are we going, Felix?' she asked, not minding, so long as she was in his arms.

'Home,' he replied, and she gave a sigh of satisfaction.

When they were within a couple of kilometres from the villa, Spiro broke out into song, a romantic song, he afterwards told them, which he rendered in a surprisingly beautiful tenor voice. He deposited them with due ceremony at the gates, and full of emotion, wished them both much happiness and many children.

Felix shook him by the hand and was emotionally embraced and kissed on both cheeks. Frances solved any doubt by reaching up and kissing Spiro herself, and then, giving another of his funny little bows, he donned his cap, which had materialised on the way, climbed back into the car, and drove off. His voice, raised in song, wafted back across the mountain.

'Do you think he'll be all right?' Frances asked anxiously, as they walked slowly down the path and into the villa. 'I think he must be quite tipsy.'

Felix lit a lantern and said with amusement: 'He'll be fine, don't worry—Saint Spiridon looks after his own.' He lifted the lantern high, throwing a beam before them. 'This is the main room, you'll see better in the morning. Sofia and Maria, bless them, have been working like beavers getting it all ready for us.' Holding her close, he led her through the rooms, commenting on kitchen, guest room, bedroom ... 'And bathroom!' he exclaimed triumphantly. 'Corfiotes believe baths to be unnecessary, when the sea is so conveniently placed!'

'Are we close to the sea here?' Frances asked, moving away from him to cross the bedroom and peer out of the window.

'The garden ends by the cliff edge. There's a good path down to the beach and the swimming is safe.'

Frances gazed with enchantment at the moonlight shining on the sea.

'Oh, Felix, do come and look! How beautiful!'

'Yes,' agreed Felix, his eyes upon her, 'very beautiful.'

There was something in his voice that made Frances turn, and finding the open look of admiration on his face hampered normal breathing, she covered up her confusion by asking teasingly: 'May I be the first to use your fantastic plumbing? I feel as though I have all the dust of Corfu sticking to me.'

'You may,' Felix replied, delighting in her confusion,

and making a grandiose sweep of his arm towards the bathroom door.

When Frances returned, deliciously cool and sweet-smelling in a white nightdress carefully chosen for Felix's approval, she found the bedroom empty. Moving dreamily to the window she saw a pale blur coming towards the house from the direction of the garden. A few moments later Felix came in, a towel round his neck, hair damp and his navy bath-robe casually tied round his middle. In his hands he carried a bottle and two glasses.

'Felix, you haven't been in the sea!' she exclaimed worriedly.

He shook his head and smiled, teeth shining whitely in the dim light from the lantern.

'No, my love, I've been using our more primitive methods of taking a shower. There's a well in the grounds, with a convenient bucket! Ice-cold water, but very refreshing.' He held up the bottle. 'And Spiro, bless the man, remembered the champagne I asked him to keep cool for me.'

Frances laughed in delight. 'Where? In the well?'

'Naturally,' he told her solemnly. 'Where else?' He placed the glasses on the table and expertly popped the cork, pouring out two measures and handing her one of the glasses. Taking the other for himself, he stood looking at her before raising it to hers.

'To us,' he said softly.

'To us,' echoed Frances, taking a sip, savouring the cool liquid appreciatively. 'Mmm ... lovely, lovely champagne.' She took another sip, a more generous one, and eyed him over the rim of her glass. 'Is *this* the time and the place, Felix?' she asked demurely, a smile playing on her lips.

Felix drained his glass and reached out to take hers, disposing of them with deliberation.

'If it's not, I damn well want to know why,' he proclaimed with grim amusement, and took her into his arms. He kissed her fiercely, hungrily. 'You little wretch! To turn the tables on me so completely!' He threw back his head and laughed deeply in his throat. 'I can see you now,' he observed with a groan, 'sitting on that seat in the garden, your hands held primly in your lap, suggesting calmly that I take you away with me! If the earth had opened up and swallowed us both I couldn't have been more astounded—more horrified!'

'But why?' asked Frances, laughing quietly at his revelation.

'Why? I'll tell you why, my girl!' and he scooped her up and carried her to the bed where he settled her in his arms, her head resting on his chest. 'Because I wanted to shake some sense into you! Tell you not to throw yourself away on a man like me! The gall rose in my throat —how I'd had the devilry to suggest it in the first place was now incomprehensible to me,' and he buried his face in her hair and held her even closer.

'You were so grim I thought you didn't want me any more,' she said lovingly, cupping the nape of his neck, running her fingers up and down through his hair, savouring the sensuous feeling of delight this gave her, satisfying a long-felt desire to do so.

'Oh, I wanted you all right, but not on those terms, not like that! Not for a long time like that! I wanted to claim you for my own, harness you with the shackles of respectability, tie you to me irrevocably, so that everyone knew you belonged to me!' His lips moved warmly to the curve of her neck and he punctured his words with caressing kisses. 'I came away from that wretched luncheon feeling low and depressed, knowing the mess I'd made of apologising to you. You were so remote and uninterested, not my warm and generous Frances. What a fool I was, I told myself over and over again, that having once found the woman whom I could love and live with for the rest of my life, I have to bungle everything so abominably! I was convinced that I'd lost all chance of recovering myself in your eyes again!'

'Foolish, foolish man!' Frances murmured, nestling comfortably in his arms. 'Even when I was hating you, I knew I was powerless to stop loving you—and how ruined were your chances you must ask Gareth, for he witnessed the way I reacted to the news of your accident—hardly the actions of an uninterested person!' She paused and added softly : 'When did you first guess that I loved you, Felix? I tried so hard to hide it from you.'

'Oh, it was a conglomeration of things, my love, which taken separately meant nothing, but which put together added up beautifully ... once I knew that you'd turned down the Stoppard play. That was the final, blinding revelation. Then I began to ask myself, would you have been so angry over my wrong accusations had you been completely uninterested!' His voice took on a smiling quality. 'You should have asked yourself why I was so blazingly angry too, for the same reasons.' He took her hand and held it to his cheek. 'And then Gareth confirmed my amazing suspicions. In a moment of weakness I confided in him my feelings for you, and he told me how upset you'd been ...'

'Oh! and I asked him not to!' protested Frances feebly.

'He felt he had some justification in breaking that promise, my dear, mainly for the welfare of his patient —me—who was likely to fade away and die ... of a broken heart.'

'Nonsense,' she whispered, brushing her lips against the warmth of his shoulder. 'You wouldn't *ever* have given up ... not having that Ravenscar arrogance of yours! Now admit it! I bet you were going to be somehow involved in the Stoppard production if your acci-

dent hadn't put paid to that!' She twisted round and
smiled triumphantly, knowing she was right by the look
on his face. 'You see! You were going to hunt me down
and use your abundance of charm to get back into my
good books!' She slipped her hands beneath the robe and
curved her arms round his back, holding herself close.
'And you would have succeeded,' she said huskily, feeling his heart beating rapidly against her body. He loves
me, she told herself dreamily, basking sensuously in the
unbelievable knowledge. She had always known that
beneath the well-controlled façade there was a wealth
of passion and feeling waiting to be unleashed, and
somehow it seemed that she was the one to have released
this love! Even now, matching heartbeat for heartbeat,
kiss for kiss, it was difficult not to believe she was dreaming! and she offered her thoughts to Felix shyly, her
voice full of wonderment.

His dark brows rose, mocking her tenderly, and his
hands moved over her possessively. 'If you're dreaming
then so am I, and so long as we wake together ... in this
bed, that's all that matters!' His smile broadened. 'And
my mother must be in this dream too, because I have a
letter for you in which she sends her very dear love.'

'Oh, Felix! Really?' exclaimed Frances, forgetting her
rosy-cheeked confusion and lifting her face to his. 'Is she
too disappointed at not being here for the wedding?'

He shook his head. 'She couldn't have flown out, in
any case, because of her health, and for us to go off
quietly and do it without any fuss suited her fine. She is,
of course, convinced that it's all her own doing!'

'Without any fuss indeed!' It was Frances's turn to
tease now. 'I suppose you call flying Zoe and Gareth
out a normal thing to do? Or proposing to me in a bus!
And as for keeping me at arms' length ever since we
arrived—well! If that had gone on much longer there
jolly well would have been a fuss! It's a wonder I didn't

end up a nervous wreck!' she complained laughingly. 'I was so mixed up—I thought you didn't want me any more.'

'You are wholly adorable,' said Felix, 'and you knew darned well that I wanted you!' Giving her a little shake, he groaned: 'Oh, what a trouble you've been to me, Frances, right from the moment you stepped into that fateful lift!'

Frances gave a sigh of satisfaction and traced his profile with a light finger. 'I remember I looked across the space between us and thought what a dangerously attractive man you were!' Her lips quivered with laughter. 'And all you could do was to look down your nose at me and be horrible!'

'Nonsense,' he replied firmly, smoothing the curls away from her forehead and searching her face, eyes dark and intense. 'I looked across and thought—now there's a real beauty! and as my interest deepened and our paths crossed more and more, I found I was having to make myself resist your attraction ... your smile that demanded a smile in return, your outrageous sense of humour, your courage and generous spirit.' He shook his head sadly. 'I was a doomed man that day in the lift, had I but known it.'

Frances slanted him a wicked glance. 'I wonder what the stars say for Scorpio today?' she asked slyly, holding back from him to see his face.

Felix lifted her up and swung her round, his expression tender as his eyes hungrily searched her own.

'Never mind the stars. *I* say we have some unfinished business to attend to.' His hands dropped from her shoulders, moving down her arms to clasp her fingers in his. 'We were interrupted this morning ... do you remember, Frances, my love, my very own dear love?'

'I remember perfectly,' she murmured, 'just perfectly,' and her arms crept round his neck. With her lips very close to his, she whispered: 'Shall we ...?' but her question was abruptly cut off as Felix brought his mouth down on hers, crushing her to him. At this precise moment, words were unnecessary.

Frances Ravenscar stepped into the lift and smiled at the other two occupants already there. The doors closed behind her and the lift began to descend from the eighth floor. Frances ignored the man and woman in the opposite two corners and thought about what Tom Deverell had just told her—that she had a good chance for a part in the Shakespeare season coming up. Dear Tom, he had become a good friend ... still joking that he had been instrumental in bringing Felix and herself together and that he had witnessed their first kiss, which indeed he had. Frances' lips curved in a reminiscent smile as she remembered the anger that kiss had inspired, and how she had heartily disliked the donor, a tall arrogant fellow with yellow-brown eyes! And here she was, married to him! Even after eighteen months she couldn't get over the surprise she felt when someone called her Mrs Ravenscar, as Tom's secretary had just done.

The prospect of working in Shakespeare again was appealing ... it would be nice to finish with an old favourite. Felix would be pleased for her.

Finish ...

She smiled again, hugging her other news to herself. Felix would be pleased about that too! She glanced at her watch. In two minutes she would be meeting him ... and the thought brought a tinge of colour to her cheeks.

The lift stopped at the next floor and then continued its descent. Frances glanced at the newcomer and gave him an interested appraisal. Her regard was returned with a boldness that deepened her colouring, and she was thankful when it passed on to the blonde girl in the other corner, who was also eyeing him up and down. Frances couldn't blame her. He was worth looking at, and he knew it too, as shown by the return of his eyes upon her. The best thing to do with this situation is to do a bit of out-staring, thought Frances, but when his left eyelid dropped in a wink she wanted to laugh. The cheeky thing, and her a married woman!

Controlling the impulse to smile, she turned her attention to the fourth person in the lift, a thin, sandy-haired young man who didn't seem interested in anyone. A much safer person to contemplate, decided Frances, and began thinking about the evening ahead.

Felix had wanted to take her out to dine, but she had insisted on preparing the meal herself. This particular birthday, Felix's thirty-eighth, was going to turn out to be a special one and she didn't want to share it, or him, with anyone, not even anonymous strangers in an hotel dining room. November the second—and she hadn't even had the chance to say 'happy birthday' properly yet, Felix having had to leave so early that morning. She had merely murmured the words lovingly as her arms had left the warmth of their bed and wound themselves round his neck as he bent to kiss her goodbye. She could still evoke the fresh, newly-showered smell of him and the funny sense of loss as his weight left her, could feel his lips brush her bare shoulder and hear the tender amusement as he unwound her arms and declared firmly that as much as he hated leaving her he had a living to earn and would meet her at four at the studios.

Frances flicked a quick look at her watch—it was right on four o'clock—and gave a satisfied sigh. Everything had worked out beautifully as planned. She hadn't rushed. With her new sense of serenity she had kept her two appointments, both fulfilling her hopes. She would tell him first about her meeting with Tom, and then, when they were full of good food and wine, she would tell him that she had been to see Gareth.

She hugged the anticipation to herself and with a flicker of surprise found that her gaze had wandered back to the newcomer who was regarding her with open interest.

She found herself answering his smile, she just couldn't help it, and then the lift came to a sudden jolt, descent halted, and after a general regaining of balance, the four occupants looked at each other.

'Oh, no!' the blonde exclaimed. 'Are we stuck?' and her eyes passed round the group to finish hopefully upon the newcomer who was leaning in the corner of the lift, a resigned hand over his face.

'Does it do this very often?' Sandy-hair asked generally.

Felix lifted his head. 'Only when the stars foretell,' he intoned prophetically, moving indolently to the button plate and stabbing at the alarm bell. He then crossed to stand in front of Frances, hands flat on the wall either side of her, and eyed her appreciatively up and down.

'If you're frightened,' he said softly, using his most seductive voice, 'don't worry. I'll look after you.'

Frances could see the amazed look on the other two faces and a bubble of laughter exploded inside her. He was outrageous, he really was, but oh, how she loved him! She gave a tremulous smile and fluttered her lashes.

'Why, thank you, that is kind.' She looked down with maidenly modesty. 'I feel better already,' she confessed.

'Good,' soothed Felix. 'Perhaps I'd better hold you, in case things become a little rough,' he suggested, ably following words with action.

'Do you think shouting would be any use?' the blonde asked Sandy-hair feebly, but he was too fascinated by what was going on at the other side of the lift to answer.

Felix looked down at Frances, eyes brimming over with love and laughter, and she sighed happily, a comforting warmth spreading over her as his arms tightened their grip. And in that moment she knew that she couldn't wait, that she had to share her good news with him now, and lifting her face to his, whispered:

'In seven months it will be June.'

Felix accepted this statement at its face value, giving a quick, if rather puzzled nod of assent.

'And isn't it a coincidence, Felix, that Gemini, depicting twins, is the Zodiac sign for June?'

His brows rose fractionally. 'It is?'

'Uhuh ... because Gareth says that twins are often hereditary and we should be prepared for ...'

The lift gave a shudder and began to descend and by the time it stopped and the doors opened to allow two of its occupants to make a hasty exit, the other two were oblivious to anything but themselves.

Don't miss any of these exciting titles.

Complete and mail this coupon today!

Harlequin Reader Service

IN U.S.A.:
MPO Box 707, Niagara Falls, N.Y. 14302

IN CANADA:
649 Ontario St., Stratford, Ontario N5A 6W2

Please send me my FREE Harlequin
Reader Service Catalogue.

Name _____

Address _____

City _____

State/Prov. _____ Zip/Postal _____

ROM 2308

Don't let this chance pass you by!

Harlequin Presents...

The beauty of true romance...
The excitement of world travel...
The splendor of first love...

3 GREAT NOVELS

Harlequin brings you a book to cherish ...

three stories of
love and romance
by one of your
favorite
Harlequin authors ...

JOY
ROMANCE
LOVE

Harlequin Omnibus
THREE love stories in ONE beautiful volume

The joys of being in love...
the wonder of romance...
the happiness that true love brings ...

What readers say about Harlequin Romances

"I can't imagine my reading life without Harlequin."

J.L.,* Sioux Falls, South Dakota

"I just read my first three Harlequins. It is Sunday today, otherwise I would go back to the bookstore to get some more."

E.S., Kingston, Ontario

"I'm really hooked and I love it."

M.S., Richmond, Virginia

"Harlequins help me to escape from housework into a world of romance, adventure and travel."

J.R., Glastonbury, Connecticut

*Names available on request